Every morning wh... path by the lake, p... the long-drawn-out ... blend with the palac... on Lake Rashmi and ... But today there was n...

Disappointed, she w... urge her mare forward when a tall figure emerged on an adjoining balcony. At first she did not recognise Julian Lindsay because he was dressed in informal Indian costume; loose white trousers and a long collarless shirt.

He smiled. 'The sitar strings need tightening. That is why there is no music this morning.'

Caroline's cheeks were flushed. 'Yes,' she confessed. 'I missed hearing it . . .' Brushing aside her shyness, she asked, 'Who plays the sitar?'

'I do, of course.'

Somehow Caroline could not reconcile this new aspect of the Resident with the aloof Englishman astride his charger on the parade ground.

Lindsay was quick to interpret her unspoken thoughts. 'People are not always what they seem, Miss Emerson . . .'

Angela Morel was born in India and educated in the United States and England where her father was posted on diplomatic assignments. By profession she is a civil servant, but also devotes time to writing books on history and literature. So far she has published seven books on these subjects. She lives in Bangalore, India, with her husband (also a civil servant) and a sixteen-year-old son. CAMELLIAS FOR CAROLINE is her first Masquerade Historical Romance.

CAMELLIAS
FOR CAROLINE

ANGELA MOREL

MILLS & BOON LIMITED
15–16 BROOK'S MEWS
LONDON W1A 1DR

CHAPTER
ONE

CAROLINE EMERSON entered Vijaypur as the first light broke over the hills and spilled its glory on the impregnable fortress of greyish-pink stone. The carriage drove over the cobbled road and stopped before the richly embellished gateway—the Sun Gate—where the guards spoke to the driver and then waved him on. The horses cantered past the crenellated walls and battlements of rough-hewn stone and down the slopes leading to a broad plain.

There, in the sunshine, the Vijaypur Lancers were engaged in morning parade, marching in full regalia to the tune of a military band and bagpipes. Riding at their head on a black charger was a man in white uniform. Authority and self-assurance was stamped on his bronzed face.

When the carriage slowed down to pass the imperious figure in white, he turned to glance at Caroline. She was held by the brilliant blue eyes which assessed her swiftly; her wind-blown auburn hair, sparkling green eyes, the delicate but well-defined face and travel-creased clothes. An enigmatic smile briefly lit his stern face and, before Caroline could react, he urged his horse forward. She stared after him, strangely disturbed by the magnetism she sensed. The carriage bowled over the smooth road until it stopped before the high wrought-iron gates of the stately palace of Vijaypur.

Caroline was helped down by uniformed guards, while retainers in crimson and green livery appeared to take her luggage. A court official escorted her along the gravel path to a pillard portico and then to a long veranda onto which opened many rooms. In one of these she was invited to tidy herself and then wait until she was summoned. Before she could collect her thoughts, the official returned to say, 'The Maharaja will see you now.' She got up at once, smoothing out the voluminous folds of her skirts, and followed the man, who held open a massive sandalwood door to the Maharaja's informal audience hall.

It was an oblong room, with brocade sofas on either side, and polished mahogany tables holding priceless *objets d'art*. In the middle of the floor were several rich-hued carpets. A mingled scent of incense and tobacco drifted in as Caroline walked slowly towards the opulently dressed man sitting on a higher sofa. She sank in a curtsy before him, murmuring, 'Your Highness.'

'Welcome, Miss Emerson. Your arrival has been eagerly awaited,' the Maharaja said in a lazy drawl.

As Caroline rose, she studied the ruler of Vijaypur. Kedar Singh was about fifty, but he looked older. A life of dissipation had left its imprint on his once handsome face, while self-indulgence had thickened a figure that had once been supple and wiry. His somnolent eyes took in the details of the demure young Englishwoman standing respectfully until he waved her to a seat. 'Yes,' he thought with a touch of amusement, 'they will approve of her . . . My chief wife, my son and heir, and the interfering Resident. She looks most respectable—quite unlike her delectable predecessor.'

'I hope you will be happy here, Miss Emerson, though I cannot imagine why a person from London should wish to come so far away,' he said with a sigh.

Before Caroline could make a suitable reply, a young man sitting near the draped window remarked, 'Perhaps Miss Emerson, like others of her race, favours adventure and . . . romance.' Caroline glanced at him, and was aware of a malevolent gleam in his eyes, which were not unlike the Maharaja's; the words, though innocent enough, sounded sinister.

As a crimson flush stained Caroline's cheeks, she protested, 'I have not come in search of either adventure or romance, but simply to earn my living.'

The Maharaja waved his plump jewelled hand. 'Take no notice of my son, Miss Emerson. He is inclined to be impertinent. Well, make yourself at home,' he said, hiding a yawn. He had done his duty in meeting the governess, and now he wished to turn to more pleasing matters. 'If you need anything, see my Private Secretary.' His tone of polite dismissal indicated that the audience was at an end. Caroline rose, and dropped a curtsy before leaving. The Maharaja acknowledged her homage with a slight inclination of his turbanned head, while the young man looked at her with narrowed eyes.

It was with a sense of relief that she emerged into the cold morning air. The opulent room, the Maharaja and his unpleasant son had made her feel unsettled and increased her growing sense of solitude. Everything was exotic and alien. A feeling of panic was slowly overcoming her, but she mastered it with a visible effort, admonishing herself to be sensible and to remember why she had come so far from home.

How far away London seemed in this princely state in the western part of India! Six months ago Caroline had not known of its existence, and now she was standing in a veranda not far from the ruler's audience hall. She looked around her as the inexplicable panic subsided, and had to admit that the view was impressive.

The veranda was lined with huge brass pots containing blooms of every kind, and a series of shallow steps led to a long gravel path through velvet green lawns and formal flower gardens arranged in geometrical patterns. In the centre of the larger flower-beds were fountains and statuettes of nymphs and nereids sporting in glittering sprays of water. Tall trees of different species encircled the grounds like verdant sentinels. Now, in late winter, tiny buds of purple jacaranda blossoms were beginning to peep from new foliage. On one side the lawn disappeared into a lightly wooded area, while on the other it skirted a large lake where a small villa of luminous pink marble seemed to float like an enormous lotus. The villa was, in fact, called Lotus Mahal.

'It's all very beautiful,' Caroline thought to herself, 'and I shall try to settle down.'

Another official emerged from one of the numerous rooms lining the veranda. He was an elderly man with a tired but kindly face. 'Miss Emerson, I am Chunilal, Secretary to the Maharani. I shall inform you of your duties and timetable. But that can wait. I hear you have been travelling since early morning from Ajmer.'

'Yes, it's been a tiring journey. I should be glad to rest and change.'

A slight wave of his hand brought forward a retainer. 'Sonawala here speaks some English, so I am assigning him to you. He will run your errands, while two women, who also have some of your language, will attend to your personal needs. After you have rested, I shall take you to meet the Resident Saheb, and then your pupils.'

Caroline thanked Chunilal and followed Sonawala through corridors and staircases until they came to a quiet part of the palace. The apartment assigned to her was in a new wing, directly above the classrooms of the Maharaja's children. Sonawala threw open the door and bowed. Caroline entered and drew in a deep breath of pleasure, for the room was lovely. There was a canopied bed with upholstery of shimmering pastel silk; several vases were filled with winter flowers; a low fire burned in the marble fireplace.

'It is suitable?' Sonawala asked, puzzled by her silence.

'Eminently suitable!' Caroline enthused. 'Thank you!'

He bowed, and left. Two maidservants appeared from the sunlit corridor and began unpacking Caroline's trunks, arranging cupboards and drawers, while she sat quietly on a chair, trying to orient herself to this new life.

It was not a life she had ever planned or imagined; it had come about through a sudden and dramatic change in her existence two years earlier. Until then, Caroline had been the pampered daughter of a wealthy shipping magnate. Her widower father had given her an excellent education and brought her up to be his friend, confidante and in some ways the son he had never had. Caroline ran his home in Bayswater, kept the country home in Devon to which they normally went in summer, entertained his friends and colleagues, and travelled in Europe with him. She was twenty-one when she had met the handsome Edward Lockwood at a party in London. He was a new experience in her sheltered and sedate life.

Educated and accomplished, Caroline did not,

however, have much practical wisdom. Completely sheltered in the comfortable and secure world created by her father, she assumed that everyone was as straightforward as herself. So when the Honourable Edward Lockwood began his skilful wooing, she had responded spontaneously.

Edward had much to recommend him: good looks, suave manners, an aristocratic background and the possibility of becoming an Earl if his brother died without an heir. Caroline was naturally flattered that a dashing member of London's *jeunesse dorée* should want to bestow his attention on her—there were after all prettier and more patrician débutantes to choose from—but she was not surprised when he proposed to her at a society ball. In her world a gentleman who courted a young lady did so only with honourable intentions, and only if he loved her.

Nevertheless she was naïve enough to ask him, as they sat together in an empty terrace, 'You are quite sure you wish to marry me, Edward?'

He smiled beguilingly at her. 'Of course I do! I fell in love with you at first sight,' he said softly, caressing her cheeks in a manner that made Caroline uneasy. He was so handsome, with his fair hair, grey eyes and regular features. 'I adore you, Caroline . . . can't you understand that?'

She shook her head in wonder. Men like Edward, she felt, could adore only women as gay and entrancing as himself. But he began kissing her fingers one by one, assuring her of his eternal enslavement.

Caroline had returned home in a state of excitement, and burst into her father's study, with Aunt Hester and Cousin Geraldine at her heels.

'Papa!' she cried, flinging her arms around Cedric

Emerson. 'Wish me joy! Edward has asked me to be his wife!'

He stiffened. 'Edward Lockwood?' he asked in a subdued voice, his arm around Caroline.

'Yes,' she murmured.

Slowly he released her, frowning. 'You have not known him long, Caro. How can you be certain that his feelings are deep and . . . lasting?'

Caroline sat down, a small frown between her brown eyebrows. 'Why else would he wish to marry me, Papa?' she asked with what seemed to her as irrefutable logic.

Cedric Emerson sighed and sat opposite her, gazing at the fire dying in the hearth. His sister Hester also seated herself, and it was her presence which inhibited him from speaking plainly, a decision which affected his daughter's life profoundly. Indeed it was Aunt Hester who rebuked him. 'Really, Cedric, you might show more enthusiasm about Caroline's success and your acquiring a possible future Earl for a son-in-law!'

'I want Caroline to be happy, and it is not necessary that she has to become a Countess to be so,' her brother replied with asperity.

'He is handsome, charming, and . . .' Aunt Hester faltered. Even she, whose home was in suburban Wembley, knew that the Honourable Edward Lockwood was not rich. In fact, his father, the Earl of Elverston, was heavily in debt.

Hester and Cedric exchanged significant glances and Caroline, normally sensitive to the sublest nuances, was too much in the grip of excitement to grasp their meaning or the reason for her father's unaccountable hesitation.

'Tomorrow he is coming to call on you, Papa,' Caroline announced happily.

'So soon?'

Caroline was perplexed. 'But of course! How can we announce our engagement unless you give your consent?'

'Suppose I ask you to wait?'

She was really bewildered now. 'But why, Papa?'

'Just to be certain that you are . . . really attached to this young man,' he said steadily.

Caroline laughed. 'Oh Papa! Is that your only reason? For a moment I actually thought you might not like Edward!' Her relief was obvious. She rose from the armchair and kissed her father gently. 'Of course I am certain I like Edward!' she said, and then paused. 'You do like him, don't you?'

Cedric Emerson wished later he had spoken out then, and saved his daughter from the heartache that he knew awaited her. Yet in the face of her eager, triumphant, gladness he could not utter those crucially wounding words.

'Let Lockwood come tomorrow,' he said, prevaricating. 'We shall discuss the matter and give it all due consideration.'

Caroline laughed merrily. 'By all means!' she said, and went to her room, a little amused by her father's doubts and brushing aside the little ripples of her own uneasiness.

The Honourable Edward Lockwood presented himself the next day. Cedric Emerson saw at once why even his sensible daughter had become enamoured of this man. Nothing in her extensive education and sheltered upbringing had prepared her to resist the onslaught of so consummate a charmer. If Emerson had not known of the Lockwood family's finances, he might have had brushed aside his reservations about the marriage. But he had made his own fortune by hard work and his wits, and recognised the fellow for what he was—a persuasive hedonist. However strong his attraction for an innocent and unworldly girl of twenty-one, her father could only ask them to wait.

'Wait, sir?' Edward asked in a hurt voice. 'But I wish to marry Caroline before the season ends, and take her to our family seat in Berkshire.'

'I understand your impatience, Lockwood, but I want my daughter to get to know you better. As it is, you met only a month ago.'

Edward smiled pityingly at Emerson. 'Sir, time is of little importance. I think,' he said with a far-away look in his eyes, 'I loved Caroline from the first moment, and knew somehow that we were destined for each other.'

Emerson felt his impatience rising. 'If destined you are, nothing can prevent your marriage, but until a date is set for the announcement of your engagement, I want you to give Caroline time to reflect, quietly and soberly, for several months.'

Edward spread his hands in resignation with such good-natured acquiescence that even Emerson felt the first stirring of qualms. 'Very well, sir, I shall take myself off to Berkshire as soon as the season ends,' he said courteously. 'You will permit me to write to Caro, I trust?'

This was proving more difficult than an international transaction, and Emerson's lips tightened. 'Occasionally . . . and, if I may say so, not fulsomely.'

Edward revealed his perfect teeth in a delighted laugh. 'Sir! What an ordeal you have set me! But I shall respect all your wishes. And at the end of this ordeal-by-waiting may I come to London in the autumn and announce our wedding date?'

As Emerson nodded assent, he was wondering, as he gazed at the fair-haired, grey-eyed Adonis, whether he had been unfair and unjust. Was it not perfectly natural that an innocent, unspoilt and refined girl like Caroline should stir a man's heart, regardless of his rank or wealth?

It was a fateful summer. Emerson's fortunes met with serious reverses because of the Civil War in America. The sinking of two of his ships prompted investors to remove their capital and entrepreneurs to choose a more devious shipper who would deal effectively with the American patrol boats.

He cut short his country sojourn in an attempt to stem the tide of disaster. Caroline accompanied her father, and wrote to Edward to tell him of the misfortune that had overtaken them. Edward did not reply at once, but when he did, it was to voice doubts about their compatibility. 'You are too intelligent and sensitive for a person like me. I begin to feel unworthy of you and wonder if we can be happy together.'

Caroline understood at once that Edward did not wish to marry her now. Proud and impulsive, she wrote back immediately, breaking off their engagement. It was a dismal autumn day, and she stood by the window, shaken by his behaviour.

By the time her father returned home that evening, she was calm and collected. He had enough problems, she decided, without adding to them. But soon he came to know what the young man had written, and was not unduly surprised but deeply pained to see how Edward's conduct had affected his beloved child. The depth of her disillusionment was not concealed by her outward

composure. Emerson saw that she would hencefor-
ward question the values she had been taught to
cherish.

In order to try to forget the bitter knowledge that she
had been fooled and humiliated in swift succession,
Caroline immersed herself in her father's business
papers. The transition from trust to disenchantment was
not easy, and had the effect of changing her from a naïve
and trusting girl to a woman sceptical of people's
motives. She resolved never to fall in love again.

Her father was sad to see the change in her. One cold
winter evening as they sat by the fireside he assured
Caroline that one day she would meet a man worthy of
her: 'Someone who will value you for what you are and
who will not give a damn whether you are an heiress or
an impecunious woman.'

'Are there such men, Papa?' Caroline asked quietly.

Emerson realised that the question itself revealed
her new-found cynicism. 'Of course there are. I am
one such. I married your mother although she was
the daughter of an impoverished parson and I the pos-
sessor of a shipping fortune. Oh yes, my child, one
day you will meet a man who will be worthy of your
dreams.'

Six months passed, six months of anguish as father and
daughter accepted that they were no longer well off.
They grew closer than ever in this new ordeal and
cheerfully planned how to cut their losses. For both, the
cheerful façade was a pretence. Emerson bore the bitter
burden of his financial failure and his daughter's unhappiness. In the end, worn out by so much anxiety and
heartache, he gave up the struggle and died quietly in his
sleep.

Caroline found herself completely alone. It took three

months to sell off the two houses and the other remaining assets to redeem her father's debts. Paintings, silver, porcelain, tapestry and most of her mother's jewellery had to go. As autumn was setting in, Caroline went to live with Aunt Hester and her family. Those very people who had been the beneficiaries of Cedric Emerson's success and wealth now became cold towards his daughter. Aunt Hester never stopped complaining about the cost of keeping a genteel lady like Caroline in comfort; she was at her cousins' beck and call, and they taunted her continually about Edward. In a year, Caroline changed from a carefree and happy girl to a quiet, withdrawn person.

Then she wrote in desperation to a friend of her father in India, whom she had met in London. Hugh Merton had been a partner of Cedric Emerson at one time, but then he left England to become the owner of a fleet of ships plying between India and the Far East. He wrote back, inviting Caroline to make her home with him and his family. She was touched, but declined politely; she wanted to be independent.

Several months were spent in correspondence, until Merton wrote, 'A friend of mine is the Resident in one of the princely states in north-western India. He informs me that a governess is required for the Maharaja's children. If you are interested, everything will be arranged. The Resident did want an older person, but I've assured him that you are very competent. You will be comfortable, and receive a good salary.'

Caroline began to make plans for the journey to India. Aunt Hester was furious because she was losing an unpaid housekeeper, and warned her of the consequences of her folly. None of this deterred the girl, who went ahead with the arrangements for her departure.

Within a month she embarked at Liverpool on a Pacific and Oriental liner to Bombay, and from there she was to travel north by train to Vijaypur.

CHAPTER
TWO

'ALL YOUR things are ready,' Pannabai, the older maid, murmured. Caroline was roused from her reveries by that voice, at once so meek and maternal. The woman joined her palms together and bowed low, as did Chunibai, her niece.

'You wish for anything else, Miss Saheb, before we prepare your bath?'

'No . . . Thank you.'

'Then we shall get your bath ready. Which fragrance do you wish—jasmine or tuberose or camellia?'

Caroline smiled. It seemed as if she had stepped into an unreal world. 'Anything you suggest.'

They filled the tub in her bathroom with scented warm water while camellia petals floated on the surface. And when she had bathed, they wrapped her in a robe, laid out her dress on the sofa and told her to sleep until evening, when they would return to arrange her hair and help her to dress for dinner. Then they were gone, their glass-encrusted skirts swinging, the bells on their ankles keeping rhythm with their footfall.

Caroline sank on to the luxurious bed. The train journey had been exciting but exhausting. After arriving in Vijaypur, she felt all the accumulated weariness of the past three months creeping over her as she glided into a deep and dreamless sleep.

A silver and rose twilight lingered on the windows before merging into a soft evening. The wind from the wooded hills above Vijaypur was sharper now, with a winter's edge. Caroline opened her eyes and could not place her environment immediately. Then everything came back, and for a moment she felt a sudden panic rising to her throat. Why had she left the dreary safety of Aunt Hester's house for this frightening new world? The two maids walked over to the bed, bells jingling, and smiled.

'Miss Saheb had good rest?' Pannabai asked.

'Oh yes.'

'And now we get you ready.'

Caroline allowed them to plait her hair which she wound round her head, selected a high-necked green taffeta dress, designed by Worth in the days of her father's affluence, and put a string of large pearls around her neck. She stood back and smiled at herself in the mirror. Yes, she looked very demure and sedate, as should a governess in an exotic oriental court.

Shortly afterwards, Chunilal came to escort her to meet the Resident. They walked across the palace gardens towards the Residency. Classical and compact, it stood in total contrast to the rambling, ornate palace. With its pedimented porticoes, balustraded wings, colonnaded entrance hall and Adam-style façade, the Residency, so evocative of Regency England, made no concessions to Indian conditions except for the circular veranda round the sides to ward off both the summer sun and monsoon storms.

Chunilal led her along the flower-decked veranda to the Resident's office, where a turbanned attendant in white tunic and red sash ushered her in. It was a large airy room with a wide bay window overlooking the lake, while another had a view of the colourful palace gardens. It was simply and austerely furnished. Two walls were filled with prints of old battles and a high shelf contained thick volumes of revenue statutes, criminal and civil procedure and other reference books.

Behind a vast leather-topped desk sat an impressive man wearing a light grey suit. Caroline recognised him at once as the man she had seen riding at the head of the Lancers early that morning. She dropped a curtsy and murmured, 'Your Excellency.'

Sir Julian Lindsay stood up and asked, 'Miss Emerson?' Then, indicating a chair opposite, said, 'Please sit down.'

Caroline sat down, straight backed, with hands folded on her lap, trying not to be intimidated by the piercing blue eyes that appraised her carefully.

'Mr Hugh Merton spoke highly of you,' he said abruptly and without preamble. 'And it is on his recommendation that I agreed to your appointment.'

'Thank you,' Caroline murmured, wondering how he managed to make a compliment sound derisive.

'However, I should tell you that I did it with some reservation.' Caroline's finely arched brows were raised in a mute query, but the Resident continued. 'You are first of all too young for the position and have absolutely no previous experience in this profession. Neither have you any knowledge of India . . .'

'I have done some reading on the voyage from England,' Caroline said defensively, her cheeks warm with indignation.

'Excellent,' he said in a sardonic tone. 'Presumably you will now be better equipped to deal with Indians, their culture and customs. Your immediate predecessor had no idea of these, and treated her sojourn here like a holiday and adventure.'

'I assure you, Your Excellency, I have not come with that intention,' Caroline said coldly while the colour on her cheeks deepened with anger. It was unfair of the Resident, she felt, to treat her like a frivolous adventuress when he must know of her background and education.

'I am reassured to hear that, Miss Emerson, because the situation in an Indian princely state is not the easiest one to handle. It calls for tact and understanding along with firmness. I hope you will do nothing to embarrass the British Government, and that you will always remember you are an unofficial emissary of your country. Any graceless or undignified action will be as much a slur on your country as on you. It is something which we cannot afford . . . not now, when we are just settling down after the upheavals of the Mutiny.'

He paused, and for a moment Caroline thought a dark shadow flitted across his face, as if the Mutiny of 1857 over ten years ago, conjured up painful memories.

'The British have an important role to play in India, Miss Emerson. We have come not only to extend our territories but to spread the best traditions of our country—justice, fair play, rule of law. If these values can be woven into India's ancient values, we can mould a great country. Each one of us has something to contribute.'

Caroline was moved, despite her dislike of his hauteur. 'I shall do my best,' she said gravely. The Resident rose, and Caroline realised that the audience was over.

He bowed stiffly. 'You can start your duties tomorrow, Miss Emerson. Today you are to meet the Maharaja's family.'

Caroline dropped a brief curtsy, murmured 'Good evening', and walked towards the door which was held open by a red-coated, turbanned attendant. Pensively Lindsay watched her go, wondering what sort of person she was and how she would respond to India. Then, with a shrug of his shoulders, he turned to the despatches on his desk.

Caroline walked in silence next to Chunilal through the Residency gardens towards the palace grounds. She felt curiously agitated. Hugh Merton had assured her that she could rely on the Resident in this alien land, but she felt that he was even more cold and forbidding than the Maharaja and showed not the slightest inclination to be a friend. He was the Resident, the *de facto* ruler of the ruler of the princely state, and looked down at her from his lofty position.

The visit to the zenana or ladies' quarters was almost a diversion after the encounter with the Resident. The Maharaja's womenfolk lived separately there, observing purdah and seldom meeting any man outside the family circle. If they ventured out, they were heavily veiled so that the lascivious glances of other men would not profane their flesh. The Zenana was in the western wing of the rambling palace. As they passed through the marble halls touched by a lilac light, Caroline questioned Chunilal about the evening programme. He explained that as this was her first evening, she would dine with the Maharaja, the Maharani and the eldest prince and princess.

Entering the main hall of the zenana, Caroline was overwhelmed by its opulence. It was decorated in oriental style with thick carpets scattered over the veined marble floors, low brocade sofas, tables of ebony and ivory, silver lamp-stands encrusted with semi-precious stones and Rajput miniatures on the walls. A huge silver statute of dancing Shiva was in one part of the room, and flowers and incense had been offered there. About twelve women of different ages were sitting on the sofas, shimmering in silks and glittering with jewels.

The courtier led her to a pale plump lady wearing a brocade sari and several necklaces. 'Your Highness, this is Miss Caroline Emerson, the new governess,' Chunilal said in Hindi, and murmured to the English girl, 'This is Maharani Sitadevi, chief wife of the Maharaja.'

Caroline curtsied low before the Maharani, whose sad hazel eyes rested briefly on the young woman. Caroline sensed a melancholy spirit in her. Chunilal then introduced her to three other ladies—all concubines of the Maharaja, and the eight princesses.

These family details she had been told by Hugh Merton, but in London it had all seemed unreal. Now, face to face with the royal concubines and their progeny, Caroline felt bewildered. She remained outwardly composed, sipping a glass of sherbet as she watched the ladies and they watched her, wondering if she would be like her flighty predecessor.

It was finally Princess Padmini, daughter of the chief Maharani, who took the initiative to sit next to Caroline.

'Miss Emerson, you seem very surprised,' she said in careful English.

Caroline turned to the Princess, who looked a younger version of the faded Maharani Sitadevi, but instead of her mother's sadness, Padmini had a piquant gaiety that bubbled over despite the rules of sedate behaviour.

'Surprised? No . . . I am . . . just a bit overwhelmed.'

'Admit it. You are shocked. Yes?' Padmini asked, and two dimples appeared on her cheeks. Caroline shook her head unconvincingly, gazing at the lovely, mischievous girl.

'They all are in the beginning,' Padmini said ironically.

'They?' Caroline asked.

Padmini nodded, eyes sparkling, 'All the governesses and tutors from England who have come and gone.'

'I see.' It was a sobering thought for Caroline.

'One even tried to become a Maharani.'

Caroline wondered if she were being warned not to harbour such designs. Suddenly she felt angry. 'That must have been some time ago—when your father was much younger,' she replied recklessly.

Padmini laughed. 'So you think my father is too old? Well, look discreetly at his fourth wife. Yes, the one to my mother's left. She is seventeen years old—the same age as I. My father married her two years ago.'

Caroline put down her sherbet. She felt slightly sick.

'But of course, she is not a Rajput,' Padmini said contemptuously, not of the aged man who had married a child but of the child forced to wed an aged man.

At that moment the door flew open and a resplendent young man strode in. He was wearing a pale cream silk *achkan* or high-necked coat. His turban was also of cream silk, with an enormous ruby in the centre. It could have been the Maharaja twenty-five years ago, but the Crown Prince was slim and supple, possessing almost a sinuous grace. On his entrance, all the wives except the oldest hastly pulled the *anchal*, the loose end of the sari, over their heads.

Sitadevi glanced tenderly at him as he came towards her, bent down to touch her feet and then kissed her jewelled hands. 'What brings you here, my son?' the Maharani asked.

Prince Kamal Singh smiled. Caroline saw that he had the same dimples and mischievous sparkle as Padmini.

'I have come to see Miss Emerson,' he announced in English. There was a suppressed giggle from the cluster of women and girls. Caroline rose slowly to her feet. Kamal Singh advanced towards her, one hand extended for a handshake.

'Will you make my sisters into little mem-sahebs, Miss Emerson?' he asked.

Caroline dropped a deep curtsy. Then, looking directly at him, she said, 'I hope to teach them only as much as a governess can. I have no authority to go beyond the curriculum.'

Prince Kamal smiled and nodded. 'I hope you open up their horizons,' he said. Then, after a pause, he added, 'You have to be particularly careful with my sister Padmini. She is somewhat headstrong.'

Padmini pouted at her brother. 'Are we not all?'

Caroline refrained from joining in the exchange, but her expressive green eyes betrayed all her doubts and fears.

'And now, Miss Emerson,' the Crown Prince announced, 'I have the pleasure of escorting you ladies to dinner.'

Caroline waited for Sitadevi to lead, followed by Padmini. She noticed that the three other wives slipped away to an inner room, to dine with their daughters. Padmini explained that the concubines did not dine with men outside the family, and Caroline did not ask who that man might be.

She knew who he was, though, when they entered the western-style dining-room. It was rich and ornate, with heavy rosewood cupboards and side tables elaborately carved. A damask-covered table stood in the centre.

Four gold candelabra gleamed over it, while yellow roses floated on chased gold bowls. Silver cutlery and English china were formally laid out.

Almost immediately, the Maharaja came in through another door, followed by the Resident and several courtiers. Greetings were exchanged between the courtiers and the princely family. The Resident introduced Caroline formally to the courtiers, but did not address her beyond a 'Good evening, Miss Emerson.' They took their seats: the Maharaja at one end of the table, with Sir Julian Lindsay and Prince Kamal on either side, while the chief Maharani sat at the other end between Princess Padmini and Caroline. Along the sides sat the courtiers and Prince Pran Singh, the son of the second Maharani who had been present during Caroline's audience with the Maharaja.

It was a rich and sumptuous meal; western cuisine mingled with Moghul dishes and a generous choice of wines, filling the room with the exotic aromas of saffron, cinnamon, beaten silver, crushed pistachio and the subtlest herbs.

Caroline ate sparely, her healthy appetite subdued by the excitement of the setting in which she found herself. As this dining-room was not the main one and used by the Maharaja only for small informal dinners, the table was not large. Caroline could therefore see everyone and hear their conversation. She had the uncomfortable sensation that the Resident was subjecting her to a relentless scrutiny with those brilliant sapphire eyes, so startling against his bronzed, clean-shaven face. He looked as much at ease in his elegant evening dress as he had in his grey suit or military uniform.

He watched Caroline's pale and delicate face illuminated by warm candlelight, and her auburn hair seemed to reflect the flames of the candles. Her luminous green eyes were veiled, and Sir Julian Lindsay found himself glancing at them, wondering what lay hidden in their depths. However, when Caroline asked Princess Padmini why the other princes and princesses had not joined them for dinner, the Resident said tersely, 'That is the custom here, Miss Emerson.'

Nettled by his peremptory tone, Caroline replied softly, 'Customs can be changed, I suppose, your Excellency? It might be a good idea for them to dine together.'

A strange silence fell upon the table. The Maharaja, who had been talking desultorily to a courtier, fixed his hooded eyes on the two English people. The Resident sensed this at once, and thought of ignoring her remark. But he was not accustomed, after ten years in India, to having his views questioned. 'What is good, Miss Emerson,' he said evenly, 'you can evaluate only after you have been here long enough to assess the situation.'

Caroline was delighted to see that she had provoked the Resident, and would not stop now. 'It would seem an innocuous enough innovation,' she said lightly, glancing around her with an innocent smile, but was surprised when she found Princess Padmini frowning at her plate, her cheeks aflame.

Pran Singh emitted a low laugh not unlike a growl. 'You will find nothing is innocuous here, Miss Saheb,' he said in that unpleasantly smooth voice.

Prince Kamal smiled across the table at her. 'Miss Emerson, you and I must discuss the latest educational ideas current in England. I became interested in them while I was at Oxford a few years ago.' He then turned to the Resident. 'Do you remember the gentleman, Julian, who believed that caning was damaging?'

Padmini and the Maharani relaxed, as though a potentially dangerous topic had been averted by Kamal.

Lindsay did not reply at once. His eyes were on Caroline, defying her to contradict him again. She turned away from his gaze, trying to answer the polite questions put to her by Sitadevi.

When her eyes returned once more to the Resident, they rested on his left hand, where a gold wedding-band encircled his third finger. 'So he is married,' she thought, wondering where his wife was. 'In the hills or in England? Or maybe she has run away from his tyranny?' The idea made her smile ironically, and when she looked at him, she found that he had intercepted both her glance and her smile, for he looked reflectively at his left hand before removing it from the table.

The Maharaja rose, stifling a yawn. Once more he had done his duty and was bored. He led the way out, followed by everyone else in order of precedence. The gentlemen waited to greet the Maharani and Padmini who, followed by Caroline, walked towards their wing.

Once more back in her room, she went to open the window and found the Resident walking across the illuminated palace gardens towards his own brightly lit house by the lake, his head slightly bent as if he was trying to solve a riddle.

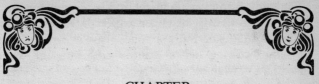

CHAPTER
THREE

CAROLINE WAS awakened by birdsong from trees that reached up to her window. They were songs she had not heard before, so she sat for a while on the marble window-ledge to listen to the deep, sweet chants. After a while Pannabai came in, her full skirts swaying, glass bangles tinkling, bearing a tray full of exotic fare. Caroline drank a cup of fragrant tea, nibbled at a thin crisp cake and a jewel-like pomegranate, and then went to take her bath. The maid had strewn the water with camellia leaves and petals.

'Princess Padmini says you're like a camellia—so this is to be your flower,' Pannabai explained the extravagance of the toilette. Caroline felt herself warming to the whimsical and charming princess, hoping that her other charges would be half as pleasant.

She met them in a light airy room with latticed marble windows overlooking a courtyard where flowers and fountains glittered in the sunshine. Seven of the princesses glided in, ranging from sixteen years to five, all wearing the Rajput costume of voluminous skirts sewn with tiny mirrors, short silk blouses revealing apricot-hued skins and a gauzy veil wrapped loosely around their torsos. When they married, the veil would cover their heads. Their slender wrists glittered with thin gold bangles, their ears sported exquisite pendant ear-rings while silver anklets kept rhythm with their steps. Caroline smiled at them and they at her. They had never had such a young governess, and had already decided to take advantage of her youth. Sensing this, Caroline made it clear that she expected obedience and diligence or she would have to report them to their father.

The girls listened in awe, and then to prove their earnestness bent over their books. Caroline put the older girls into two groups, and proceeded to teach them the prescribed subjects. She wondered what had happened to Princess Padmini and why she had not yet appeared. Of course Padmini was seventeen, she thought. Surely she would have received some education by now.

For three hours she taught the girls, gave them their homework, and was preparing to leave when she became aware of a sari-clad figure standing by the fountain in the courtyard. Another person was with her, a slender young man in a dark suit. His back was turned, but Caroline thought he looked like an Englishman. Just then, as though they had become aware of her scrutiny, the young man and Padmini turned. Caroline did not avert her gaze, and after a moment, Padmini walked towards the classroom. The young man followed her.

'I was expecting you, Princess,' Caroline tried to sound professional.

Padmini nodded. 'I know—but since Richard . . . er . . . Mr Brooke . . . was free, I took some time off.' She introduced them, and added, 'Mr Brooke is tutor to my brothers.'

Caroline surveyed the young man. He was slim and of medium height with brown hair and light blue eyes.

'I am pleased to meet you, Miss Emerson,' he said in a pleasant voice, and shook her hand.

Caroline inclined her head. She felt a natural affinity to the young man who had also come so far to earn his livelihood. Padmini watched them for a moment and then said brightly, 'If your classes are over, Miss Emerson, may we go to your apartment for some tea?'

Caroline was about to refuse, but she saw a plea in Padmini's eyes which she could not ignore. Besides, the Princess's request could be construed as a command.

As the classroom was in the same wing as Caroline's apartment, they went up quickly by a flight of pink marble stairs. Caroline ordered tea and lemonade and invited her guests to be seated. She was aware of a special relationship between the two people which made her uneasy.

Nevertheless she engaged Richard in polite conversation and learnt that he had studied Oriental History at Oxford and had come to India to deepen his knowledge. Since his family was not wealthy, he supported himself by teaching the Maharaja's sons while continuing his research in Rajput history, and then planned to return to England to teach.

While he was speaking, Padmini looked pensively out of the windows, and then she said quickly, 'Miss Emerson, I hope you and Mr Brooke will be friends.'

Caroline glanced at the Princess and then at the English tutor. Her surmise was confirmed. 'Naturally we must get along, since we are going to work in the same place.'

Padmini looked soberly at Caroline, and said, 'In fact, Miss Emerson, we shall rely on you . . . to meet here. You and Mr Brooke could also organise joint classes for my brothers and sisters. I can then spend more time studying.'

For the first time Padmini seemed like a princess:

imperious, determined to have her own way. Caroline began to feel uneasy. 'I shall . . . have to . . . discuss this with your mother,' she parried.

'The Maharani does not decide these things,' Richard said. 'You will have to clear it with the Resident.'

Padmini made a face, 'And we know how sympathetic he is!'

'I shall speak to the Resident,' Caroline murmured, her uneasiness increasing.

'Have you met him yet?' Richard asked.

'Oh yes, they have met,' Padmini interposed with a smile. 'And they do not look as if they will be the best of friends. But then, His Majesty is imperious with everyone.'

Caroline smiled. 'Why do you call him "His Majesty"?'

'Because he is more powerful than my father.' There was a faint resentment in Padmini's tone.

Caroline could well understand her resentment. After the Indian Mutiny, the business of ruling India had passed from the East India Company to the Government at Westminster. While the British Government directly administered the three Presidencies comprising the major provinces, a special relationship was evolved between the British Crown and the feudal states ruled by Indian princes. These princes, who carried the titles of Maharaja, Raja or Nawab, were largely autonomous except in matters of foreign and economic policies. While according the Indian rulers every honour, the Government appointed 'Residents', who functioned as observers and advisers to the princes, but were responsible only to the Viceroy of India. Their role required both firmness and understanding, tact as well as authority. They were inwardly resented by the rulers, who nevertheless tried to make the most of the situation.

After they had finished their tea, Richard left, followed by Padmini, who paused at the door and smiled her thanks.

Caroline sat down and gave a deep sigh. Had she bargained for all this when she came out East? No, it had merely been an escape from monotony and misery, from humiliating memories of Edward Lockwood's rejection and the tragic one of her father's death. She had hoped to find peace and anonymity in India instead of this growing tension she sensed around her.

That day passed quickly. Caroline lunched with the princesses, and Richard with the princes, followed by a siesta and more lessons. The afternoon was rose-gold when she returned to drink tea in the solitude of her room. The dinners were like the luncheons, but with greater formality in dress. In the little drawing-room set apart for the teachers, Caroline and Richard had coffee together and discussed the homes they had left behind. Caroline listened as the tutor spoke of his plans. She did not feel like revealing her past to this stranger. But he was a pleasant young man, and in her new surroundings she welcomed his cheerful company.

A few days passed in this manner. Caroline began to rise early to savour the matchless beauty of the north Indian winter mornings. There was a sharpness in the air and glittering dew on the grass, while the sun rose behind Devgiri Hill, splashing the marble palace with light turning the flowers and trees to flame, and it was reflected in Lake Rashmi, which lay still and serene under the shadow of the hills.

Every morning when Caroline rode on a chestnut mare along the bridle-path by the lake, past the Resident's house, she heard the long-drawn-out strains of

Indian music. The first time, she had passed by without stopping, but subsequently she paused to hear the sighs of the sitar quicken into a tremulous joy. The music, so different from her beloved Chopin and Liszt, seemed to blend with the palace, the temple atop the hill, the villa on Lake Rashmi and the winter blue of the Vijaypur sky. Caroline wondered who played the sitar with such verve and sensitivity. The alien music had begun to communicate to her something of India, of a spirit that lay hidden behind ceremonies and forms. It was also as though the sitar spoke to her, hinting at secrets and promises yet to be fulfilled. She regularly pulled up to hear the music before galloping to the forests at the foot of the hills.

One morning she was waiting near the window from which she heard the music, but there was no sound. Disappointed, she was about to urge her mare forward, when a tall figure emerged on an adjoining balcony. At first she did not recognise the Resident because he was dressed in the informal costume of north India: loose white trousers and a knee-length collarless shirt embroidered in front with cream silk.

'Missing the sitar this morning, Miss Emerson?' he asked pleasantly.

'Oh . . . Good morning, Your Excellency,' she murmured, embarrassed at being found so close to his windows. 'I was . . . on my way up to Devgiri for a ride.'

He smiled, ignoring her explanation. 'The sitar strings need tightening. That is why there is no music this morning.'

Caroline's cheeks were flushed, despite the sharp morning chill. 'Yes,' she confessed, 'I missed hearing the sitar . . .'

'I know. I see you stop and listen every morning. Do you like Indian music?'

Julian Lindsay looked at her red-cheeked face and into the depths of her emerald eyes, touched by a new awareness of her person.

Brushing aside her shyness, she asked, 'Who plays the sitar?' In her mind she had already conjured up a dark-eyed Indian damsel entertaining him.

'I do, of course.'

'Really?' Caroline asked, astonished. Somehow she could not reconcile this new aspect of the Resident with the aloof Englishman astride his charger on the parade ground.

Lindsay was quick to interpret her unspoken thoughts. 'People are not always what they seem, Miss Emerson,' he said gravely, never taking his eyes from her questioning face. 'Each of us has different dimensions in our existence.'

Caroline nodded, her gaze moving away from him to the glassy surface of the lake, conscious of a strange new sensation tugging at her. They stood for some moments in silence and then he looked up at the hills.

'The sun will be strong soon, Miss Emerson. Let me not detain you from your ride. I would ask you to join me for a cup of tea, but, since you are not chaperoned, I must forgo the pleasure. No doubt one morning you can come escorted by Princess Padmini.'

His tone at once alerted Caroline, dragging her from the strange new mood which had enveloped her. She looked at him uncertainly.

'Come now, Miss Emerson, you know what I mean,' he said easily. 'Be less eager to play the duenna to the Princess, and she might then be less tempted to meet Richard Brooke.'

Caroline was taken aback that he knew of their occasional rendezvous in her room after classes, and was unsettled by the mild rebuke in his voice. She touched her mare's flanks gently with her heels. 'I shall remember, Your Excellency,' she said unsteadily. 'And now, if you will excuse me, I shall continue my ride.'

He nodded, gravely eyeing her tense face. Caroline rode swiftly away, trying to suppress the sudden misery which had replaced the vague happiness she had felt by the Resident's balcony.

To avoid any more encounters with him, she gave up riding past the Residency and now followed the opposite bridle-path by Lake Rashmi, sometimes gazing upward to Devgiri Hill to see the young sunlight glinting on the spires of the temple dedicated to the goddess Parvati. The sunbeams moved on and touched the light and graceful summer palace called Mahadev Vilas not far from the temple. It was like a miniature Taj Mahal, with four slender minarets and a central cupola. It had been built two centuries earlier by a Maharaja of Vijaypur who had admired the Moghul emperor's architecture, if not his policy.

Padmini began to accompany Caroline in the morning. The Princess introduced her to the costume of north India—loose trousers or *shalwar*, a loose tunic called the *kameez*, and the gauzy *orni* with which the head was covered. It was on these rides that Caroline came to know much about Rajput customs and traditions and the role of Vijaypur in the turbulent history of Rajasthan.

Also on these excursions she learned about the intrigues of the second wife of the Maharaja to designate her son Pran Singh as heir to the throne by setting aside Prince Kamal, son of the chief Maharani.

'Fortunately the Resident supports my brother, but even then the concubine will think of something,' Padmini murmured, glancing around for eavesdroppers.

Caroline shook her head. 'The second Maharani can't do anything illegal—there are laws of inheritance,' she assured her pupil.

'Oh, Miss Caroline, there are so many ways of evading the law . . . poisoned sherbet, a scorpion under a pillow . . . a trap in the forest when the men are on a *shikar* . . .'

'Come now, Princess, it can't be so bad!' Caroline said, trying to shake off a vague disquiet caused by the girl's foreboding.

'That is why I want to leave Vijaypur. Will it not be nice if I can run away with Richard?' Padmini asked softly.

Caroline abruptly reined in her horse, causing the animal to neigh shrilly in protest. 'That is rather an extreme solution, is it not, Princess?'

'Not really. You see, Sir Julian and my brother want me to marry an old Maharaja—a widower at that. I'd rather commit *johar*!' she announced theatrically.

'That is the custom of self-immolation, isn't it?' Caroline asked, horrified.

'Yes! My ancestress and namesake, Queen Padmini of Chitor, did it rather than submit to the Sultan of Delhi. I shall keep up the tradition if I am forced to marry the old Maharaja!'

'You must not say such things, Princess,' Caroline admonished her pupil.

'I shall not threaten any more, Miss Emerson, if you would plead my case before the Resident. Will you?'

'I shall consider the matter,' Caroline parried.

'It will not be easy,' Padmini warned. 'You see, Sir Julian had an unhappy marriage, and so has little use for romance.'

'Has he?' Caroline asked, urging her horse forward. 'Well, I'm sure he will be sympathetic to you.'

She did not hear Padmini's reply because her thoughts were far away from the Princess. She was back in England, amid the glittering social events of a London season, with the Honourable Edward Lockwood beside her murmuring endearments. 'I too have been dis-illusioned,' Caroline thought as she rode through the sun-dappled woods, 'but I have not become as aloof and indifferent to others as Sir Julian.'

Indeed Caroline had been disappointed by his critical attitude to her. Hugh Merton had assured her that the Resident would be a friend in the new environment. Instead, he had turned out to be quite different. She realised that he was intelligent and efficient, respected and feared, but he maintained a wall of reserve around himself.

Curiosity to know more about him prompted Caroline to ask Richard Brooke about the Resident when they met for tea after both had finished lessons with the children.

Richard admired the Resident, whom he had known since childhood as the two families had adjoining estates. Julian Lindsay came from a family with a long tradition of service in the army and administration. He had read philosophy at Oxford and had been decorated for valour in the Crimean War.

Richard paused in his narrative to look at Caroline, who was listening intently. 'At that stage Julian could have stayed on in the army, where a bright career awaited him, or stood for Parliament, as his father had done. Instead he decided to go to India.'

'Why?' Caroline asked.

'Well, he had come across the writings of the famed

jurist Sir William Jones, who became a great expert on Indian civilisation. The careers of Elphinstone, Metcalf and Tod in India also inspired him to follow their examples. He came here to learn of India's ancient culture and to introduce the best in the British heritage.'

Caroline glanced out of the window at the gardens, beyond which the Residency glowed in the late afternoon sunlight. 'Why is he a Resident, then? Surely he should have chosen a scholar's path?'

Richard shook his head. 'In India, an European scholar would have no authority. He has to be in a position of power. Julian joined the East India Company, fought in the Mutiny and then worked in the office of the Viceroy, Lord Canning, who was so impressed by his work as a scholar and administrator that he recommended a knighthood. Julian was knighted at the age of thirty-two. Thereafter the Viceroy sent him to Vijaypur as Resident.'

'I sensed at once that he was very intense and dedicated to his work,' Caroline observed.

'Indeed he is. He has already written several books on Indian history.'

'He plays Indian music, too,' Caroline mused, remembering the haunting and evocative tunes she used to hear in the mornings. She paused, remembering also the narrow gold band on his ring finger. 'He is married, is he not?' she asked, with hesitation.

Richard was at once uneasy. 'He was . . .' he said quietly.

'Padmini told me that he was unhappy . . .' Caroline faltered, colouring.

'I believe so . . . I never had the courage to ask him what exactly went wrong.'

Caroline nodded, gazing at the fountains glittering in

the twilit gardens. 'Is that why he has immersed himself in his work?'

Richard shrugged his shoulders. 'Perhaps. I doubt it, though. I think Julian loves his work and is absorbed in his dreams for India. No woman would find it easy to compete with such an obsession, and poor Priscilla certainly could not.' He paused, a rueful smile on his face. 'Perhaps that is why he is a little intolerant of other people's . . . emotional problems.'

Impulsively Caroline said, 'Never mind, Richard. You must be master of your destiny.'

Inwardly she realised that, far from being a friend, Sir Julian Lindsay would be a critic, satisfied only by efficiency.

'I shall not disappoint him,' Caroline determined firmly as they parted for the day.

CHAPTER
FOUR

THE LAST vestiges of winter disappeared as the jacarandas and laburnums burst into bloom. Clusters of purple and yellow flowers blossomed by Caroline's window, while birds came to nest there and fill the air with their twitter. One morning she awoke to find the lawn in front of her window filled with people wearing old clothes which bore smears and splashes of colour. Their faces were smudged with blue, vermilion and yellow powder. She could not distinguish anyone in that strange masquerade, though familiar voices cried out to her to join them. As she stood bewildered by the window. Pannabai came to her and smiled. 'Today is the festival of Holi, to welcome the spring. You must go down in an old dress and take part in the games.' While Caroline dressed, Pannabai told her about Holi.

In ancient times when Lord Krishna lived on this earth, he met his beloved, Lady Radha, in a scented mango grove on the night of the first full moon spring. It was a day when social barriers were forgotten as everyone celebrated with coloured water and powder.

When Pannabai had finished, Caroline went down to the lawn in an old cotton dress, her hair tied into a loose knot. The faces of the revellers were hardly distinguishable as they pressed forward in the games. She thought she could get glimpses of several of the concubines, who flouted purdah at Holi. She could also distinguish Richard Brooke, whose light hair and eyes betrayed him. Caroline eagerly joined in the merriment of splashing coloured water at the revellers and getting drenched with colour herself. After a while she went to a fountain to rinse the coloured water from her eyes before joining the revellers.

As she was doing so, a tall figure in colour-splashed clothing advanced towards her. His hair was powdered green, his faced smudged with purple and yellow powder. Coming up to her, he smiled, and said in the grave voice so well remembered, 'You have enough colour on your face, Miss Emerson, so I shall only put a *bindi* on your forehead.' He inscribed a small red dot on her forehead with his forefinger, then stood back to see the effect, and said, 'You look just like a Hindu lady with the *bindi*.' His dark blue eyes took in her disorderly appearance with a wry smile. Her auburn tresses had freed themselves from the prim knot and hung to her waist in cascades, touched here and there with coloured powder. She held his eyes for a long moment and for a while the laughter and revelry did not reach them. Then abruptly the Resident moved away to join Prince Kamal, who was having the most riotous time of all.

Caroline stood still, bemused. Was it because the ritual of putting a *bindi* on a woman's forehead was done by no man other than a betrothed or husband? And did Julian Lindsay, so well versed in Indian customs, not realise the significance of this gesture? For Caroline something irrevocable had happened, something to which she dared not put a name.

The revelry ended late in the morning and everyone went to bath and change. Not all the colour disappeared.

Patches of green and vermilion still clung to hair, arms and cheeks.

As Holi takes place in the time of the full moon of Phalgun between February and March, an evening of music had been arranged on the main lawn with court musicians playing the tender-toned sitar, the deeper sarod, the rumbling tabla and the plaintive tanpura. A separate area had been reserved for the ladies, and it was there that Caroline sat with Princess Padmini behind Sitadevi and three concubines. Now and then she stole glances at Lindsay, who was placed next to the Maharaja and Prince Kamal. He was now wearing western evening dress, looking very much the British Resident. He too glanced at her and smiled appreciatively. She could clearly make out his strong chiselled features, his eyes closed as he listened to the *Kafi* raga dedicated to the spring. The alien music plucked at her own heart-strings, stirring up strange longings which she was not prepared to acknowledge to herself.

After the music and dinner, Padmini asked Caroline to walk with her by the lake. The lakeside looked so beautiful in the golden moonlight that she agreed, despite her misgivings about the walk. They set out about ten, when everybody had retired to their rooms and the retainers were at their meals. When they came to the lakeside, Padmini indicated a shallow boat lying on the still waters. 'We shall row a short distance, and go to the little villa in the middle of the lake,' she whispered. By now, Caroline was caught up in the strange, restless mood that had been growing since the morning. She agreed, and the two women sat in the boat while a slim turbanned man sprang to row them out to the villa. Lotus Mahal had been a favourite retreat of the Maharaja in his youth. Here he had organised his revels and splashed in the lake when the carousing ended. He did it, he said, not to offend his Maharani by conducting orgies in the palace!

The water dripped like pearl droplets from the oars as the boat glided towards the villa, gleaming above the water. As they reached the marble steps, the boatman helped the Princess out, and then Caroline.

Recognising him, she gasped, 'Richard! You should not have come!'

'Of course I shouldn't have! But I am here and no one is the wiser,' he chuckled.

Padmini laughed softly. 'So you guessed, Miss Caroline? I'm glad! I should hate to deceive you!'

Caroline was disturbed by the situation. 'You should not have done this, Princess,' she said in a tone of disapproval.

Padmini pouted. 'Well, I have! And no one will guess—unless you tell them!' she retorted, and then used a gentler tone. 'You won't, will you, dear Miss Caroline? You know how much I long to be with Richard!'

Caroline had not the heart to rebuke her further. 'Well, all right. Just for a while, then. After that we must return to our rooms,' she relented.

'Thank you, dear friend,' Padmini said, squeezing her hand as she and her beloved disappeared to one of the terraces above.

Caroline felt suddenly very old, playing the duenna to an irresponsible princess and the nonchalant tutor. Sitting in the pavilion, she gazed across the moonlit lake at the palace, where the lamps were being put out one by one. Her eyes strayed to the pillared portico of the Residency, which stood dark against the moonlight. 'Is he also sitting like me and thinking the same thoughts?'

she wondered. Quickly she reproved herself. The Resident was an aloof, self-contained person, preferring solitude to society, the mysteries of this vast country to the sparkle of London life. He had shut himself out from human contact. Yet the memory of his cool finger on her forehead evoked a strange tumult in her. She was still wearing the *bindi*. Had he seen that?

Lost in these thoughts, she did not see a boat glide up to the pavilion. It was only when the tall figure stood on the marble steps that Caroline emitted a startled cry.

'Enjoying the moonlight all by yourself, Miss Emerson?' Julian Lindsay asked in a strangely subdued voice.

Caroline felt her heart pounding madly. Had he come to join her? She looked up at him and saw the answer to her question in his eyes. All joyous expectations vanished.

'I . . . that is . . .' Her voice died in her throat.

'Well? Are you alone or are you playing the duenna to the two fools?' The Resident's voice was like a whiplash, though his eyes rested briefly, almost tenderly, on her forehead.

Caroline bowed her head, and murmured, 'Yes.'

'I expected better sense from you.' As always, his chill rebuking tone roused her ire.

'Why? Am I not doing the correct thing to chaperone the Princess? Would you rather she came alone?' she asked, equally coldly.

His lips tightened. 'I would rather she did not come at all,' he said grimly.

'Your Excellency does indeed rule the lives of his subjects!' Caroline said tauntingly.

'Don't speak of matters beyond your understanding!' he snapped back.

By now Caroline was really angry. 'Why do you begrudge that girl a little joy? Is she supposed to be cold and inhuman like you?'

'Inhuman?' he echoed in a harsh tone. 'You think I am inhuman?' With these words the Resident moved swiftly forward and pulled Caroline roughly to him and bent his head to capture her lips.

For a moment she was too stunned to react. Then she felt a wonderful warmth flooding over her body as she yielded to that crushing embrace and the demanding mouth which sought her cool, trembling lips with such urgency. Her hand moved to his neck, while his hands caressed her cheeks and hair. Then, as Caroline felt she was drifting into the moonlit sky, Lindsay abruptly released her. 'Forgive me . . .' he said hoarsely. 'I . . . am not myself today.'

Caroline stood forlorn. But pride came to her rescue. 'You are forgiven,' she replied shakily. 'It is the moonlight.'

Lindsay took a step forward, as if to protest that the moonlight had nothing to do with it, but he too was governed by pride. 'I think it's time we left. Please call the Princess and Richard,' he said in a barely audible voice.

Still trembling, she went to call the two, who came to the front of the pavilion, horrified to find the Resident. Caroline expected Lindsay to express his anger, but he did not do so.

Instead, in a sad and weary voice, he said. 'The Princess should return with Miss Emerson . . . I shall come later with Richard in the other boat. It would be disastrous for Padmini to be seen with Richard at this hour.'

Padmini came slowly forward, and tentatively took

the Resident's hand. 'I am sorry, Sir Julian . . .' she
began, but he turned away.

'You have caused enough drama for tonight. I shall
speak to you tomorrow. Good night.'

The two young women slowly climbed down to the
boat and Caroline, accustomed to boating during her
Devon holidays, took the oars. They moved across the
lake to the palace, shimmering in the moonlight. Neither
spoke a word. Each was wrapped in her own thoughts.
For a while they were content to cherish the evening,
though fully aware that, when the sun rose the next
morning, they would have to face the consequences of
the evening's escapade.

Caroline waited the whole day for a summons from
the Resident. She knew that Padmini and Richard had
been called and that there had been a stormy session.
Padmini had told her little about the content of their
arguments but, whatever it was, the Princess was
subdued.

'I shall have to commit *johar* like my namesake, the
Rani of Chitor, not for my honour but to end an empty
and useless life,' she said dramatically that evening
to Caroline who sat meditatively by the blossoming
jacarandas.

'There are other solutions,' Caroline observed dryly.
'Many of us endure empty lives without going as far as
johar.'

Padmini did not stay long: she retired early with the
plea of a headache. Caroline lay awake, anxious and
unhappy, until she fell asleep from exhaustion as the
moon went down over Lake Rashmi.

CHAPTER
FIVE

SPRING IS A brief season in north India, a time between the memory of crisp days and the anticipation of the hot weather. It comes swiftly and goes as quickly, leaving behind a fragrance of flowers and the clamour of nightingales. After pouring forth her most vivid colours, nature waits in dread of the hot desert winds.

Caroline lived through the brilliant spring days with a strange restlessness. When her work with the princesses was over for the day, she sat by a fountain in a secluded part of the vast palace garden, wrapped in thoughts.

These thoughts centred upon her present dilemma. Since the night of Holi, Caroline felt drawn to the Resident even while she resisted the pull. She looked forward to seeing him, yet made every effort to avoid him. When they did meet in one of the palace drawing-rooms she became restless and agitated, finding it difficult to maintain the serene composure she always displayed. On his part, Lindsay was correct but aloof and hardly spoke to her; when he did, it was with a measured courtesy that chilled her. Yet, when she did not see him for a few days, Caroline became restless and agitated in a different way. At these times she became annoyed with herself. An inner voice whispered, *'Haven't you learnt a lesson from Edward Lockwood?'*

'Indeed I have,' she replied to that inner voice. 'I do

not believe in love—not the kind that I dreamed of, anyway. I came to India to forget the past and to earn my living in dignity. I will not let anyone disturb the even tenor of my days . . . certainly not the self-sufficient and self-satisfied Resident who is so absorbed in his work and plans for Vijaypur!'

Ironically, it was his very dedication to work that attracted Caroline to the Resident. Men with vision and determination were rare in the comfortable and leisured world she had known before her father's death. Involuntarily she compared the Resident with Edward, whose chief preoccupation was the social round, the talents of his tailor and costly courtesans. Though by birth Sir Julian belonged to the same privileged world as Edward, he had forsaken the luxury and security of English life to take up a challenge.

'He reminds one of a *conquistador* braving uncharted seas to find a new world,' she mused one evening as she sat by the lake, gazing at Lotus Mahal across the amber waters. As always, her mind returned to the night of Holi when she had melted in his arms, her lips captive to his. As daydreams began to enthrall her, Caroline suddenly rose from the flower-strewn ground. 'I must remember all that meant nothing to him. He has not spoken to me since. I must go away for a while . . . to shake off these insidious cobwebs.'

The decision to go away was reinforced by an invitation from Hugh Merton to visit them in Calcutta now that he had returned from a business trip. Caroline wrote back to accept as soon as she had obtained permission from the Maharaja's Private Secretary to take leave for a month. He made arrangements for her journey with a suitable escort, as she would be travelling right across the sub-continent.

A few days later, the Resident sent her a note asking if she would kindly call at his office after her classes were over in the afternoon. Caroline was surprised by the summons because, since the encounter at Lotus Mahal, he had avoided meeting her alone. Deliberately she did not go to her room to wash or change, determined that he should see how little she cared about her appearance before him. However, as soon as she entered the curving veranda of the Residency, she felt awkward because he stood awaiting her, impeccably dressed in a cream-coloured suit with his dark hair brushed neatly back. If he felt embarrassed, he did not show it as he led her to his office and invited her to take a comfortable armchair, seating himself opposite her.

The room was simple and austere, and she had already felt that it bore the stamp of the man who occupied it. Papers were neatly stacked in separate files and despatch boxes arranged for the day. There was one innovation, though—on the coffee-table before them stood a bowl of camellias.

As Caroline looked around her, Lindsay was pre-occupied with the lighting of his pipe. 'I hear you are going to Calcutta, Miss Emerson,' he said at last, looking thoughtfully at her.

'Yes,' she replied without elaboration.

His deep blue eyes were startling against his bronzed skin. 'Are you unhappy here or . . .' He broke off, got abruptly to his feet and stood by the window overlooking the lake, saying in a quieter voice, 'Or are you still angry over the episode on the night of Holi?'

Caroline did not reply at once. 'It is only an episode to him,' she thought ruefully.

Lindsay remained standing by the window, looking at the lake and thinking of that night. When she did not reply, he said, turning to her, 'I assure you such a thing will not happen again. Please don't leave, if that is what is bothering you?'

Caroline wondered how he would react if she told him that it was the very reason for her departure? Would he be pleased or perplexed? Well, she would never know, because she had no intention of telling him! Never again would she allow herself to be slighted.

'No, I am not angry about that,' she replied at last in a voice which she hoped was cool and indifferent, but was so sad and subdued that he came and sat by her.

'I am going to Calcutta to meet Uncle Hugh, who is your friend and was once very close to my father,' she said with more composure.

'I am glad, because I . . . rely on you, Miss Emerson,' he said with obvious relief.

'Indeed? You have a strange way of demonstrating that,' Caroline said dryly.

'Forgive me if I am impatient at times. Perhaps if I explained to you the difficulties of my position as Resident, you would be more tolerant.'

'I should be honoured if you would do so, Sir Julian, even though you once told me not to interfere in matters beyond my understanding.'

'On the contrary, Miss Emerson, I have grown to have a high opinion of your judgment. You have worked wonders with the children within a month.'

'They are the least troublesome people in Vijaypur,' she said with a faint smile.

'So you have sensed the undercurrents here?' he asked.

'I did not really sense them. Princess Padmini told me . . . of the intrigues of the second Maharani.'

'An honourable title for such a woman,' Lindsay said with unexpected feeling.

'I can hardly repeat the names the Princess uses in private,' Caroline replied wryly.

Julian Lindsay nodded. 'I don't blame her. That woman has caused so much unhappiness in her and her mother's lives.'

'The Anne Boleyn of Vijaypur,' Caroline murmured.

'Something like that. She is inciting the Maharaja to actions which would in the end be detrimental to him. As it is, the Viceroy is in favour of deposing him. He is there because I pleaded that the Kedar Singh be given a second chance.'

'What has the Maharaja done to incur the wrath of the Viceroy? He seemed too indolent to be of any danger to the British Raj.'

'Appearances are deceptive, Miss Emerson. He is certainly pleasure-loving but not indifferent to power.'

'Aren't all men interested in power?' Caroline asked, glancing significantly at the Resident. He met her quick look with a dry smile of understanding.

'Not all men, Miss Emerson. Perhaps a few do also care for what they can achieve with the exercise of power. It is a means, rather than an end in itself. Since the British came to India there have been the adventurers, as well as the idealists who are genuinely dedicated to serving India and working towards her progress.'

'Why, then, should the Indians resent that?'

'The people don't. We have received opposition mainly from the Maharajas and Nawabs who, until recently, ruled their domains with absolute authority.'

'I heard that the East India Company officers were no better,' Caroline observed warmly.

Lindsay smiled at her indignant tone. 'Of course they were not. That is why there was the Mutiny . . . because they were as arbitrary and avaricious as the Indian rulers. Both sides fought for mainly selfish ends. There were others in between who were fired by the idea of freeing India . . . for them, I have nothing but respect.'

'And yet you are a member of the British Government?'

'That does not prevent me from respecting those who have ideals of their own. We cannot rule India for ever. All empires come to an end. But if we leave India a better place than we found it, our achievements will endure. Let the *Pax Britannica* be in this age what the *Pax Romana* was in the ancient world.'

Caroline saw Julian Lindsay's face soften as he seemed to look forward to the time when India would be restored to her pristine glory.

'Unfortunately,' he said, coming back to reality, 'people like Kedar Singh would like the old order to continue so that they retain absolute authority over their subjects, bleed the peasantry white and live a life of indolence and pleasure!'

'Is the Maharaja opposed to you?'

'The Maharaja is opposed to progress and any curtailment of his despotic powers. He did not participate in the Mutiny, but supplied arms to the rebels when they seemed to be doing well. He has got rid of two Residents with remarkable astuteness. Both were demoralised by his lavish gifts and blandishments until they ceased to be independent or effective.'

Caroline smiled. 'And, of course, he has failed to demoralise you.'

'He will therefore try other means to get rid of me.'

'What means?' Caroline asked with apprehension.

The spontaneous anxiety in her eyes made Lindsay pause. *Could it be that she was really concerned?* he asked himself. 'Don't worry, he will not dare unless he gets desperate,' he said reassuringly. 'However, his resentment of me has increased since Prince Kamal entered the scheme of things.'

'How is that?'

'Kamal has shown every promise of being a modern and able ruler. In the three years I have been here, he has matured and developed sound judgment. I am convinced that he wants to serve Vijaypur, and not the other way round.'

'Prince Kamal thinks highly of you,' Caroline said quietly.

'Does he? Anyway I have tried to train him to be a modern ruler. He went to study for a few years in Oxford, travelled in England and France, studying local government, and to the Netherlands and Switzerland to study new methods of agriculture and dairying. He has great plans for Vijaypur . . . If he is not prevented from succeeding his father,' Lindsay ended ominously.

'Who would do that?'

'His father and the second wife.'

'But how? The eldest must inherit!'

'They will try to discredit him. They are doing so already by saying that he is not a traditional Hindu and that he has lost caste by going abroad. In India, that is a serious matter.'

'Can a father be so selfish?' Caroline asked, astonished.

Lindsay smiled at her incredulity. 'Fathers have been known to kill their heirs rather than let them change their policies. Kedar Singh is not only selfish; he is cruel and degenerate. Moreover, his second wife has an absolute hold over him. So he may nominate Pran Singh, the son by his second wife, as his heir.'

'Would you let him do that?' Caroline asked indignantly.

'My dear Miss Emerson,' Lindsay said gravely, 'I shall certainly try to prevent such a thing if I can. That is why I have asked Kamal to be scrupulously careful in his speech and conduct. He must not provide any grounds for the feudal aristocracy of this state to fear him as an aggressive radical.'

Caroline was listening carefully. 'I understand your anxiety.'

Julian Lindsay drew his chair a little closer to her. 'Do you, Miss Emerson?' he asked intently. 'Then perhaps you can lighten my load a little?'

'I could try,' Caroline replied softly, warmed by the entreaty in his voice and the intensity in his eyes.

Afraid of the sudden intimacy that threatened to blossom, he stood up abruptly and pressed a bell. A bearer came into the room at once. Lindsay ordered tea, then sat down again by Caroline. 'How remiss of me to keep you here at tea-time without offering you refreshment,' he said pleasantly, returning to a more impersonal mood.

Tea was obviously ready and waiting because the man returned a few minutes later with another bearer, and they set down a silver tray with silver teapot, milk-jug and sugar-basin. A three-tiered silver dish displayed paper-thin sandwiches, pastries, cakes and sweets. The bearers served them, and Caroline poured tea into the Spode cups. Lindsay watched her at this task, grateful that she neither demanded nor sought attention, neither did she make him feel uneasy by coquetry. He looked at her bent head, the late afternoon sunbeams gleaming on her auburn hair, and the slender hands at once so sensitive and capable. He took his cup from her, and sank back with a sense of strange regret.

'You were going to tell me what I could do to help you,' Caroline said, breaking into Lindsay's thoughts.

'Of course,' he said, lighting his pipe, 'Prince Kamal has, however, one problem.'

'What is that?'

'His sister Padmini.'

Lindsay's sapphire eyes rested on Caroline's face. She did not flinch from the calm scrutiny, though it quickened her pulse.

'Princess Padmini would have been married by now but for some matter connected with her horoscope. In India, most marriages are arranged after consulting the stars and planets. Since the Princess's horoscope raised some difficulties, her marriage was postponed . . . until the inauspicious effect of Mars is over.'

Caroline frowned. 'How extraordinary! But you don't believe in all this, do you?'

'Not really,' he said with a sigh. 'But I have lived here long enough to understand the spirit of fatalism. Sometimes I find myself questioning our free will.' He paused, and continued. 'Now there is an offer for Padmini from a neighbouring state. Unfortunately she is infatuated with young Brooke.'

'Are you certain it is not a genuine attachment?' Caroline asked softly.

'There is no question of taking the matter seriously,' Lindsay replied with impatience. 'Further, any gossip about their . . . romance would ruin her reputation and diminish Kamal's status in Rajput society.'

'So she must marry a widower twice her age?' Caroline asked coldly.

'Nonsense! The Princess exaggerates. If she had any sense she would be grateful for such an offer instead of being foolish about Brooke.'

'Do you believe only in marriages of convenience?' Caroline asked in a toneless voice.

'They work out better in the long run, Miss Emerson,' he said gravely, looking into the depths of her eyes. 'It takes good fortune, even a sort of grace, to experience love. Sometimes that miracle happens, but it is rare.'

Caroline felt her heart leaping: his sensitive gaze seemed to understand the turmoil within her. For a moment it seemed as if he might contradict himself. Then abruptly, as if sensing some peril, Lindsay turned away and stood looking at the garden which lay in the amber haze of twilight.

The gardeners had finished their work for the day and were splashing their faces at the fountains. A heady aroma of roses came drifting into the room. As the moment of danger passed, the Resident came back and stood before Caroline.

'Will you keep an eye on Princess Padmini and advise her against reckless escapades . . . such as on the night of Holi?' he asked in a level voice.

Caroline felt a rush of warmth to her cheeks at the mention of that night; then a chill sensation replaced it. Lindsay spoke of that night as if it had no significance for him. 'As if he often took women in his arms and kissed them wildly!' Caroline thought with rising indignation, struggling to look as unaffected as he was. But it was difficult to be calm when he stood so close to her—tall, dark and imperious.

Then, as her own sturdy pride took over, she rose from the chair and looked back at him with a defiant glint in her emerald eyes. 'I shall give whatever advice I feel is beneficial for her, and what she is prepared to accept,' she said loftily.

'That may not suffice, Miss Emerson,' Lindsay was roused by her stubborn tone. 'Please remember what I said. If Padmini does anything foolish, she will jeopardise her own future and that of her brother.'

'And your plans for Vijaypur as well, I gather?' Caroline asked with scorn.

'Yes, that too, Miss Emerson,' Sir Julian agreed softly. 'All my work will be ruined.'

A bitter smile curved her lips, darkening the sparkle of her eyes. 'I shall do my best, as long as it is humanly possible. I trust you make allowances for human failings?' she said. 'Thank you for a delicious tea. Good evening, Sir Julian.'

Lindsay's face registered no anger at her sarcasm. He smiled his whimsical smile, and murmured, 'Good evening, Miss Emerson. Thank you for coming . . . and listening.'

He watched her walk across the Residency garden, opening the wicker gate which connected his domain to the palace. The evening breeze billowed out her skirt and ruffled her hair, flame-coloured in twilight. 'Now, why did I ask her not to leave Vijaypur?' he asked himself. 'Would it not be better for all concerned if she never returned?'

'I am glad I am going away for a while,' Caroline thought as she walked to the palace. 'It will give me a chance to meet new people and revive Papa's old friendships. I must forget this man. He is indifferent to me. Nothing matters to him except his work and his plans for Vijaypur!'

She looked back, and saw him still standing on the

veranda, a self-contained, solitary figure. 'It is futile even to think of it—but the love of such a man is worth attaining!'

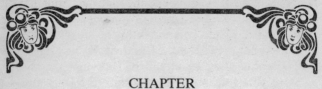

CHAPTER
SIX

PLANS FOR the Calcutta trip went ahead. The Resident personally scrutinised arrangements for Caroline's safe travel. He decided that Richard Brooke should also go, to carry detailed and confidential reports about the affairs of Vijaypur to the Viceroy, Sir John Lawrence.

Lindsay's real reason for sending Richard to Calcutta was to prevent further gossip about Princess Padmini and the tutor. If he sensed this, Richard showed no reluctance to travel—the idea of a paid holiday in Calcutta was not to be scorned. The Princess, however, wore a mournful air and confided to Caroline that she regarded the Resident as a heartless and scheming man. Caroline was ready to agree, but refrained from saying so. 'Don't worry, Padmini,' she soothed her pupil. 'We shall soon be back.'

A few days before their departure, Colonel Dalrymple, commanding officer of the Vijaypur Lancers, was the host at a dinner-party for the Crown Prince. Mrs Dalrymple sent a casual invitation to Caroline, who was so put off by the tone of the letter that she declined to accept until Prince Kamal himself prevailed upon her. 'The Colonel is a friend of the Resident. It would create friction between you and Julian if you refused the Dalrymples' invitation.'

'I dare say. Relations between Sir Julian and me could

not be less cordial,' Caroline confided to the sympathetic Prince. 'He has seldom a word of approval for me.'

The Prince sighed and shook his head, but did not encourage her to criticise the Resident. He was satisfied when Caroline agreed to attend the Dalrymples' dinner.

Along with the entire military staff, the Dalrymples lived in the cantonment area near the fortress which guarded the gateway to Vijaypur, separated from the civilian population inhabiting the Civil Lines.

Arnold Dalrymple was very different from the Resident. Bluff and genial, he shared few of the predicaments of Julian Lindsay. To the Colonel, all that mattered was the prestige of the British Raj and he would do everything to maintain it. Despite his complete certitude about the supremacy of British culture, he was prepared to be kind and just to 'the natives' so long as they did not 'get ideas unsuitable to their station'. The Mutiny had, in his mind, demonstrated what happens then, and—God help him!—he did not wish to see another upheaval of that sort ever again.

Matilda Dalrymple was ideally suited to her husband. Hardened by life in India, she had no patience with the dilemmas that plagued thoughtful Britons like Lindsay. Robust and matter-of-fact, she enjoyed her position as the *burra* mem-saheb, the senior white lady, of Vijaypur, dispensing wisdom to the *chota* mem-sahebs, the junior white ladies, and snapping orders in pidgin Hindustani to the swarms of servants.

Caroline arrived in a closed carriage with Princess Padmini, since Prince Kamal, the Resident and Richard Brooke had decided to go earlier in an open curricle. Lanterns illuminated the flower-filled gardens where the band of the Vijaypur Lancers waited in readiness to play.

There was a hush in the conversation as the gleaming coach bearing the Vijaypur crest drew up before the portico of the commanding officer's rambling bungalow. Colonel Dalrymple straightened his jacket and rushed forward to assist the ladies down from the carriage.

He and his wife considered it a signal honour that the eldest princess of Vijaypur had expressed a desire to attend their dinner, since Rajput noblewomen strictly observed purdah. Had they known that the English governess had goaded her to insist on the outing, their pleasure might have diminished. 'Wonderful of you to come, Your Highness,' the Colonel said to Padmini, who was resplendent in jewels and gold-embroidered sari. Then, turning to Caroline, he murmured, 'Good evening and welcome, Miss Emerson,' with a cordiality that surprised Caroline. He led them to the centre of the lawn, where his wife stood awaiting.

The Colonel's lady greeted the Princess effusively, but used a cooler tone for Caroline who was, after all, a mere governess. Her pale eyes hardened momentarily when they assessed the value of Caroline's ivory satin gown made by a London designer, and the double string of pearls adorning her long neck. In no time Mrs Dalrymple had drawn her own conclusions as to the how an impecunious governess could dress with such quiet elegance.

The two young ladies drew admiring stares from all the guests and, as soon as the introductions were effected, the officers of the Lancers and their wives surrounded them, eager to make their acquaintance. Julian Lindsay stood at some distance, wearing a dark evening suit with a crimson cummerbund, several decorations discreetly glimmering on his evening coat. He watched the two of them for a moment and then turned back to resume conversation with the officers around him.

As the band struck up the tune of Weber's *Invitation to the Dance*, a young woman in a white ball-gown emerged from the cluster of officers surrounding her and walked towards the Resident. Just then Caroline turned, to see her addressing him. He bowed elaborately and led her to the wooden-floored area set apart for dancing.

The Resident's partner was a Junoesque blonde with pale blue eyes, a pink and white complexion and a rosebud mouth that opened to laugh frequently. Intrigued, Caroline asked a guest next to her, 'Who is the lady with whom the Resident is dancing?'

'That is Miss Lydia Dalrymple, lately arrived from England, where she has been at school.'

'Oh! I did not know the Dalrymples had a daughter,' Caroline remarked.

'Indeed, they have two more daughters in England, but neither is as pretty as Miss Lydia.' The guest paused to look at Caroline. 'In fact, the Dalrymples expect her to make a brilliant match . . . perhaps here in Vijaypur.'

Caroline felt a leaden weight descend on her gay mood. 'I see,' she murmured.

'She will make a proper hostess for the Resident,' the garrulous lady continued. 'But, of course, the Resident has yet to declare.'

At that moment Richard Brooke came up to Caroline and asked her to dance. Grateful to escape from further gossip, Caroline accepted his invitation and was soon waltzing with other couples on the wooden floor in the middle of the garden. Out of the corner of her eyes she watched Lydia chatter and laugh with the Resident, who seemed happy in her company. Caroline felt an unreasoning anger surge within her.

'She is pretty,' Richard observed dryly. 'But not as charming as you.'

Caroline blushed, vexed that she had been so obvious in her interest in Miss Dalrymple. 'I am sure she is very charming, since she can make the solemn Resident laugh,' she replied with unwonted asperity.

When the waltz was over, Caroline returned to her seat, feeling the excitement of the evening fade. Now of course she understood why Mrs Dalrymple had been so cool towards her. She wanted no rival for her daughter's chances with Sir Julian Lindsay.

Princess Padmini and Prince Kamal joined her, aware of the sudden clouding of her spirit. They talked together until Richard joined them.

'Your Highness,' he asked Prince Kamal, 'May I dance with your sister?'

The Prince frowned. 'My sister, Mr Brooke? I do not think she knows how to dance.'

'Oh yes, she does! I've taught her the waltz and the polka. So she does know!' Richard stopped, aware that he had revealed too much in his unthinking enthusiasm.

The Prince, however, laughed. 'Well, that is certainly another matter. I do hope you will not mention this to anyone else? You see, Mr Brooke, our customs are quite different from yours. No Indian lady can afford to be seen dancing in public. Only courtesans are allowed that freedom.'

'I understand, Your Highness,' Richard murmured, reddening, and glanced at the Princess, whose liquid dark eyes entreated her brother.

Prince Kamal nodded. 'However, since we are on British territory now, I agreed to just one dance in deference to *your* customs.'

Before Kamal had completed his permission, Richard

swept Padmini into his arms and led her to the dance floor where enthusiastically they executed the steps of a polka to the amazement of everyone, especially the Resident, who abruptly left the group around him and strode to the Prince's side.

'Kamal,' he said urgently in an undertone. 'What is going on? Padmini should not be seen dancing!'

The Prince smiled. 'Miss Emerson has decided to launch my sister in western society. We might as well do everything.' He turned to Caroline. 'Now, Miss Emerson, let us see if we can do better than those two. Will you dance?'

Caroline curtsied, and without a glance at the Resident accompanied the Prince to the dance-floor. However, as she circled round, her eyes strayed more than once to Julian Lindsay who watched her intently, admiring the light grace of her movements. He was joined presently by Lydia Dalrymple.

'Not dancing, Sir Julian?' she murmured.

'I am watching the others dance,' he said absently, gazing at Caroline.

'So I see. You know, Sir Julian,' Lydia said sweetly, 'it seems that Miss Emerson inclines to be very free with the natives. I notice a degree of intimacy between her and the Princess which is quite unusual among English ladies.'

'Very unusual,' Sir Julian replied with a smile that baffled the Junoesque beauty. Then the dance ended, and he bowed to Lydia.

As the band struck up again, Caroline was invited to be the Resident's next partner. 'I will show him I am indifferent,' she told herself as she schooled herself to be composed. However, her gloved hand trembled in his firm clasp and she felt light-headed. He danced effortlessly, and Caroline felt she was floating in his arms.

Afraid of falling into the spell which he always managed to weave around her, Caroline remarked flippantly, 'You have not yet scolded me for exposing the Princess to a dinner-party and then encouraging her to dance.'

His face held some wordless emotion as he gazed down at her glowing cheeks, the glory of her auburn hair and the reckless gleam in her eyes. 'You are incorrigible, Miss Emerson. I have given up trying to exact your obedience,' he replied gently, tightening his hands on hers.

Caroline trembled, trying desperately to harden herself against the melting sensation within her. 'Indeed, Sir Julian? Have you given me up as a desperate case?' she asked in a light tone.

'I have come to accept your spirit of defiance with grace. Perhaps you understand people with a natural empathy, which is better than trying to do it with the intellect.'

He spoke seriously, and Caroline wondered what had happened to make him so benevolent towards her. Hope leapt like flames within her, extinguishing her earlier resolve to forget Julian Lindsay. He seemed to sense her turmoil, for he drew her closer.

One waltz ended and another began, but the Resident did not relinquish his partner. When the second dance ended, he invited Caroline to drink a glass of champagne with him. Offering her his arm, he led her towards a garden seat where they could talk.

But, before they could sit down, a platoon of soldiers came galloping up to the portico. Following a hurried exchange, the servants ran to Colonel Dalrymple, who motioned the soldiers to come to the front veranda, where there was a hasty consultation before he strode over to Lindsay.

Sensing that something was wrong at the approach of the soldiers, Lindsay took Caroline back to the others and went to the Colonel. 'What is it, Arnold?' he asked, taking him aside.

'Blast and damn! Bloody *badmashes*!' he muttered in rage.

'Which *badmashes* are you talking about?' Lindsay persisted.

'As if I know their heathen names! But I have a pretty good hunch that the bastard Pran Singh is behind all this.'

Calmness at once vanished from Lindsay's face, and there was a visible tensing of his frame. 'Have you any information on that score?'

'Only what my Havildar Subir Singh tells me,' Dalrymple replied. 'It seems that he was riding by when this happened, pretty casually, you know, almost like a coincidence.'

The Resident said, 'Tell me quickly what has occurred.'

Colonel Dalrymple beckoned to the Havildar, and ordered, 'Tell the men to be ready at once. We are riding into town.'

Then he turned back to Lindsay. 'They say that the grain recently harvested has been polluted by beef. They caught hold of a man who confessed to having done the deed, and beat him. When one of my Indian officers intervened, he said that it was "all untrue and a rumour spread by a miscreant".'

'Were they arrested?' The Resident asked.

'Yes—they are in the town lock-up at this moment

. . . That is, if the royal bastard has not freed them.'

'What is his role?' Lindsay asked, frowning.

'The usual stuff. The westernised Indians are ruining the purity of the caste system. He's got the crowd excited, though . . . They're threatening to burn down the jail. Shall we go, Julian?'

Lindsay nodded. 'Tell the men to carry minimum arms. I don't want any bloodshed . . . That is what the young scoundrel hopes for.'

'I'd like to run him through,' the Colonel muttered as he went to his wife.

Matilda was accustomed to such intrusions by now. Before he could tell her, she nodded and said, 'Yes, yes, Arnold, I heard. Your lieutenant told me. Are you taking all the men?'

'No, we're not taking any of your guests, Mrs Dalrymple,' Lindsay assured her. 'Just the Colonel and I and a platoon. If all goes well, we'll be back in time for supper. Now, Arnold, give me a pistol. I did not come prepared for this type of diversion.'

The Resident stopped to speak again to his hostess, and then to Lydia, who touched his arm and said, 'You will be careful, Sir Julian?'

He nodded, reassuring her with a smile.

As they were leaving the Colonel's compound, Lindsay saw Caroline standing some distance away. He went to her and said, 'Don't wait. Return early to the palace in the coach with the Prince and Richard.'

She nodded and watched him ride away in his elegant evening regalia like any cavalry officer on duty. Her spirits, revived so greatly by his conversation during the dance, now sank. She had seen the gentle exchange between him and Lydia Dalrymple.

*   *   *

When the army men reached the town, the riot was in full swing with two warring factions hurling whatever weapons they had at each other. Colonel Dalrymple rode into the thick of it. Surrounded by the crowd, his horse reared and let out a high-pitched neigh of nervousness. He flushed angrily and, instead of quietening the beast, brought his whip smartly down on the horse's sweating neck. The crowd jostled and moved closer around the Colonel, temporarily losing their fear of him.

Mounted on his horse, the Resident saw that the situation was getting out of hand. If the Colonel's horse became unmanageable, either the crowd would run away, creating a stampede, or they would become emboldened by his problem with his mount and do whatever they chose. Lindsay looked around and found that a part of the area was already in flames, set alight by those who professed to be offended by the contamination of their grain. There was no time, he felt, to argue or reason with this crowd. Drawing his pistol from the holster, he rapidly fired three rounds in the air.

The jostling and shouting stopped at once, as the crowd looked at the Resident sitting on his black charger in evening clothes, calm and unmoved by the clamour. With the pistol in one raised hand and holding the reins in the other, he shouted in Hindustani, 'Who set fire to those houses?'

There was a brief silence. Then several men pushed through the crowd, and, hands on hips, said defiantly, 'We did, Resident Saheb!'

'Why?' the query rang out like a shot.

'Because, Resident Saheb,' one man shouted, 'some low-born creature has polluted our precious grain harvested only two months ago.'

'Who told you?'

'What does it matter, Saheb? We can see for ourselves!'

'I asked, who told you? Answer me!' Lindsay said imperiously.

'We know!' the man cried stubbornly.

'I know, as well! It has been done deliberately by one who wishes to start bloodshed in Vijaypur. Have you not yet learnt to suspect those who seek to inflame you for their own ends?'

Lindsay searched the crowd for one face only, but he was nowhere to be seen. 'Why is he not here?' he shouted. 'The one who has incited you? Where is he hiding? So he is not a true Rajput after all! Rajputs never run away!'

The reaction was what Lindsay had anticipated. Pran Singh slowly made his way on horseback towards him. The crowd gave way for him with awe.

Drawing level with him, the young man said angrily, 'Of whom do you speak, foreigner?'

Lindsay's lips curled into a cruel smile of satisfaction. 'Of the coward who operates behind the veils of women, and works in the dark to ruin his own people.' He spoke slowly, so that the significance of his words would sink in for the crowd.

'Don't speak in riddles! Name the man whose birth you question,' the young man said in a high angry voice.

The Resident smiled. 'I would not foul my mouth by uttering the name of one who is neither a Rajput nor a man! It suffices if the culprit knows of whom I speak.'

He was unprepared for the next onslaught. 'And how much do you know of our people, Resident Saheb?' Pran Singh asked now in a silky voice. 'You who shut yourself up with a Prince who is your puppet ready to do your bidding and . . . a Princess who . . .'

The words remained unspoken as Lindsay once more raised his pistol and fired into the air. A palpable silence filled the area.

He drew his horse near to the Maharaja's second son. 'Enough, Pran Singh!' he said between clenched teeth. 'One more word, and you will regret it! If you wish to slander honourable people, come to the Durbar Hall before wise and learned men and make your charges there. Don't operate like a thief, behind the cloak of darkness and under orders from the zenana!'

Pran Singh flushed. His feline eyes glinted dangerously. 'I find your insinuations insulting,' he said hoarsely.

'Insulting but correct, Pran Singh?' Lindsay asked, goading him on to an act of violence or indiscretion that could ruin him.

Pran Singh sensed this at once, and essayed a cold smile. 'Yes, insult us, Resident Saheb, for we cannot retaliate. We are unarmed and powerless before the mighty British Government.'

'The British Government does not interfere in the Maharaja's domain unless the Maharaja or one of his . . . relatives fails to rule in the interest of his people.'

'Interest of the people? Are you claiming to have more feeling for my people than we do?'

'Indeed I do!' The Resident looked triumphant. The cross-fire of words had yielded results at last.

He looked at the crowd, who were now absorbed in the angry exchange between the two men. Throwing a contemptuous glance at Pran Singh, he addressed them. 'When there was a famine in Vijaypur two years ago, who brought the grain from Bengal?' he asked with a rhetorical flourish. 'Who distributed it fairly and ensured that all were fed? Do you people not remember how your Crown Prince Kamal Singh rushed back from England to share your troubles, selling his mother's jewels to pay for the grain? Where was this other noble Prince then? In a hill-station with his mother, escaping the rainless summer and evading his duties!'

There was now an eerie silence in the central square of the town. While the verbal exchange had been going on, half the platoon of soldiers had moved in and put out the fire in the three houses, while the other half moved towards the lock-up to guard Pran Singh's *agents provocateurs*.

Pran Singh was aware of the condemnation in the eyes of even his erstwhile followers. Gritting his teeth, he spoke to Lindsay. 'You win this round, Resident Saheb. But next time'—his smile was a sneer—'we shall see!' Kicking his horse, the Prince rode away.

'Go back to your homes,' the Resident said gravely to the crowd. 'And take care to think before you become the playthings of unscrupulous and greedy men.'

The crowd thinned out. The crisis was over for now, but Lindsay knew that he had brought his conflict with the Maharaja's second son out into the open. He would have preferred to have dealt with the matter in a different way, but Pran Singh had forced the issue and now there was no going back. As he watched the people dispersing to their homes, he thanked providence that the arson had been checked and contained. He had seen a minor spark like this touch off a major conflagration.

'We shall post armed guards night and day by the main grain godowns,' Lindsay told Colonel Dalrymple. 'As the warm weather sets in, the water-sources have also to be watched. They will try contaminating them next time.'

'Next time, I will shoot him,' the Colonel muttered.

'As you meant to do today, no doubt,' Lindsay replied harshly.

'Would it not have made an example of the fellow?'

'And the consequences, Arnold? Have you thought what the consequences would have been? You and I would have been branded as butchers, and recalled, leaving Vijaypur to the mercy of the very people we are opposing.' Lindsay suddenly felt very weary. Sometimes, he thought, it was not worth the effort.

'A good show of strength, a few heads bashed in and diplomacy be damned!' Colonel Dalrymple declared.

Lindsay sighed and looked up at the sable-dark sky. The Colonel's solutions, he thought, were all impulsive and never attempted to tackle the deeper issues.

They rode back to the cantonment area after posting soldiers on duty in the square and other strategic places. 'Do you suppose your good lady will have kept some supper for us?' Lindsay asked.

'Of course she has. Let us hurry home.'

Undaunted by the evening's excitement, Mrs Dalrymple had ensured that the party did not flag. The officers and their wives were just finishing dinner when the Colonel and Lindsay rode up to the bungalow, and a quick glance showed the Resident that the palace party had gone back. However, Lydia took him in hand and kept him amused with descriptions of English life.

After his return that night, the Resident sat on the veranda outside his bedroom. Vijaypur was asleep, even the guards outside the palace were silent. Millions of twinkling stars reflected Lotus Mahal in the still waters. For the first time in many years he felt weary of his solitary existence and longed for something else. What this other craving was, he could not yet formulate,

although Mrs Dalrymple had indicated what it could be
. . . a proper home and family to turn to when the
burden of work became too much.

He thought of the buxom Lydia, who was so very
different from his fragile bride Priscilla, an English rose
he had tried to nurture in an Indian garden. Memories of
meeting her at a ball crowded in on him. He had been
only twenty-five, a much decorated hero of the Crimean
War, and Priscilla was the sister of a comrade-in-arms.
She had adored him and he was swept into a mood of
romance. Both families encouraged and approved. The
Lindsays hoped that marriage would persuade young
Julian to remain in England and continue in the army
instead of going to India as a civil servant in the East
India Company. But nothing could dissuade him. When
Priscilla protested and refused to go with him, Julian was
astounded and then hurt by her lack of understanding of
his deeper interests. In the end, the nineteen-year-
old girl was persuaded by both families to accompany
him.

India fascinated Lindsay. Undaunted by the vast land
of unbearable summers and trying monsoons, he
plunged into the challenge of trying to grasp the
country—her ancient civilisation and contemporary
problems. It was not an adventure that Priscilla, a
genteel young lady brought up in a country house, could
possibly share. She found her husband's interests incom-
prehensible and became withdrawn. When the Mutiny
erupted six months later, he was preparing to send her
back to England, but she died of a virulent fever in the
long summer of 1858.

Lindsay never forgave himself for his unsympathetic
attitude to Priscilla's limitations. It was after her death
that he decided never again to become seriously

involved with a woman. His work absorbed him completely, and he grew to love and understand India.

'Why this restlessness now?' he asked himself. 'Why do I want to change things? Why should I let anyone alter my peaceful way of life? It is better as it is.'

CHAPTER
SEVEN

Two DAYS later Caroline and Richard, accompanied by Chunilal and some four servants, set off well before dawn from Vijaypur. Travelling in carriages drawn by spirited Arab horses, they stopped for breakfast at the fort town of Ramgarh, passed Sambar, the huge salt lake, and on to Jaipur, where they boarded the train in early afternoon. From the 'rose city' they sped across the plains of Rajputana to the United Provinces.

All along the route, Caroline sat watching the varied landscape: the stark landscape of Rajputana with pink and white palaces; the abandoned brown fortresses, whose ramparts once heard the clash and clamour of unequal battles between the chivalrous Rajputs and the mighty Moghuls; and craggy mountain fastnesses where proud kings once found refuge from unrelating Turkish generals. Next day they passed Gwalior and Jhansi, only recently centres of fierce Maratha resistance.

Caroline read Colonel Tod's *Annals of Rajputana*, in which the soldier-historian had explored the glorious history of the Rajputs, so that the empty forts and lonely hilltops took on a new poignancy in her mind. Tod, like Lindsay, had been the British Resident in a Rajput state and, like him, more than an administrator. She also read of the Maratha chiefs who had assumed the mantle of the Rajputs in the fight against foreign invaders, and of the celebrated Rani Lakshmibai of Jhansi, who, like Joan of Arc, had led her armies to victory until death on the battle-field claimed her at the age of nineteen.

After Rajputana the train crossed into the green Gangetic plains of the United Provinces; the stately city of Allahabad founded by the great Emperor Akbar, and Benares, the holy city of the Hindus on the banks of the mighty Ganges. They saw lush green fields, and picturesque villages with ponds of water hyacinths, where man and cattle bathed.

Caroline was fascinated by everything, and whenever she asked questions, Chunilal gave her all the information at his command. Bewildered when she had first landed in Bombay two months earlier, she had not been able to absorb much on the journey to Vijaypur. Now she could, and began to understand why this country in all its splendour and squalor had attracted people from the time of Alexander of Macedon. She read a great deal in those five days of travel, and hoped that when she returned to Vijaypur she would be able to do her work with greater understanding.

The journey was made comfortable by Chunilal's efforts and those of the servants, who served the meals brought in at major stations, cleaned and carried, and fetched hot water for their baths from the steam-engine compartment.

'We are travelling like royalty,' Caroline reflected as the three of them sat down to a typical Indian Railway luncheon when they were two hundred miles from Calcutta, pulling out of the crowded station at Bodh Gaya where Lord Buddha received his enlightenment under the Bodhi tree. Instinctively she prayed that she too might find peace and enlightenment.

'The Maharani insisted that you be looked after,' Chunilal replied warmly. He had been with the Maharani from the time she came from her father's palace in Ajmer at the age of fourteen to marry the Maharaja of Vijaypur. His loyalty, despite the advent of three more wives, was always to the gentle and gracious first wife of his master. He showed less deference to Richard Brooke, who taught the sons of the junior wives of the Maharaja. He looked at Caroline, and said with every sign of gravity, 'The Resident Saheb also enjoined me to take care of you. Brooke Saheb has been in India for some time; Miss Saheb has not.'

Late in the afternoon the train was speeding over the flat green fields of Bengal towards Calcutta. They crossed the broad Hooghly on the impressive bridge built by Sir Bradford Leslie, and steamed into Howrah station. Chunilal hired several carriages and took the English visitors to the largest hotel in Calcutta—the Great Eastern—in Old Court House Road.

Caroline was struck by the colour and elegance of Calcutta as they drove through the wide tree-lined roads. They passed the Council House, the Town Hall and the Customs Warehouse near the river. These were built in a style that sought to capture the spirit of both Imperial Rome and Regency England, with Romanesque façades, pillared porticos, and high arched windows. The only local touch was the wide verandas that tempered the heat and broke the fury of the rains. They passed the high narrow office buildings of Clive Street, the commercial heart of the commercial capital of India. Here Europeans and Indians brushed shoulders together to settle the price of tea, jute, cotton and indigo. Fortunes were made and unmade here. The Europeans suffered in their heavy western dress, for the

Indians sported loose shirts and *dhotis*—muslin cloth wrapped around their waists and swathed over their legs.

Passing the bustle of Clive Street, they entered the *maidan*—a flat broad plain with lush grass, huge trees and flowers. The Calcutta Racecourse was situated in this sylvan setting, where on Saturdays horses thundered over the turf.

At the end of the maidan stood the magnificent Government House, the seat of the Viceroy. A massive classical façade fronted the edifice, with high grilled windows and arched doors. Beyond this lay the Esplanade, where the central government offices were located.

The carriage stopped not far away in Old Court House Road, where the Great Eastern Hotel was situated. It had been opened in 1841 and called The Auckland after the current Governor-General, but had been renamed in 1865. It was expensive, but the food, service and quiet made the cost worth while.

On their arrival they saw gharries, or box-like carriages, and palanquins, resembling covered sedan chairs, lined up before the hotel, where their occupants were served the 'one rupee tiffin', comprising steak, chops, vegetables and a small peg of whisky.

Servants came hurrying out to take them to their rooms on the second floor. While Pannabai gave instructions to the hotel servants to bring refreshments and began the unpacking, Caroline stood on the little balcony adjoining her room overlooking Waterloo Street to take in the sights and sounds of the capital of British India. 'It could be Bath or Bristol,' she thought, 'except that those cities did not have the sense of space, lush verdure, the sounds of parakeets and koels clamouring

in leafy boughs or the golden sunshine glinting generously all day.'

'Well?' asked Richard, who had asked if he might
come in to see if Caroline were comfortable. 'How do
you like the Imperial capital?'

Caroline turned to look at him. 'It is an imposing city,
but entirely European in style. Why has it no Indian
buildings?'

'Because Calcutta was born out of colonial ambitions.
When Delhi and Vijaypur were vibrant cities in the
sixteenth century, Calcutta was only a prosperous village of weavers. That is what drew the Portuguese, the
Dutch and finally the British East India Company. Job
Charnock obtained permission to trade and to build a
garrison. The unsuspecting local Nawab sold him
the rights, little realising that it was the beginning of
Britain's Imperial future. The garrison became the
formidable Fort William—named after our King
William III.' Richard paused, and pointed a finger to a
wide red-brick edifice in the distance, the Writers' Building. 'Do you see that? That is now the Central Secreta-
riat, but until the Mutiny it was the office of the junior
civil servants or "writers" of the East India Company. A
British town grew around Fort William, which you see
before you.' He paused again. 'Julian first worked in the
Writers' Building until the Mutiny.'

Caroline stared around her at the stately buildings,
the broad leafy avenues, and the stream of carriages and
palanquins along Old Court House Road. It was as if the
British Raj was trying to make another London out of
the deltaic soil, lush verdure and moist heat of Bengal.

By the evening they had had their meal and baths and
unpacked their clothes. Chunilal stayed in a room near
by and ensured that they were given all due honour as

members of a Maharaja's household. He had nothing to complain of except the coffee-house attached to the hotel, where ships' masters assembled to gossip about shipping, to gamble and play billiards. Richard called in there after an early supper, but Caroline went to bed.

Next day Caroline and Richard went to pay their respects to the redoubtable Sir John Lawrence, the Viceroy.

Gone were the rough, arbitrary ways of the East India Company officers, who were adventurers out to grab the spoils of a conquered land. The Viceroy, now a direct representatives of the Crown, was invested with a dignity and authority almost as great as that of the Crown. Together with the aura of immense power emanating from Queen Victoria's representative, an elaborate system of ceremonials surrounded the Viceroy. It could be palpably felt in the ornate costumes of the attendants, and the series of officials at every layer who guarded entry to the glittering citadel of power.

Sir John Lawrence seemed to fit his rôle with the ease of a seasoned soldier and administrator who knew India intimately. Both he and his brother Henry had fought during the Mutiny, leading their side eventually to a sad and blood victory. Alongside his determination to consolidate British rule in India was a vision to serve the country.

Caroline and Richard were awed in his presence at first until he set them at ease with his bluff unceremonious manners. He received them cordially and spent a few minutes asking about their work in Vijaypur. Then the brief audience was over as further visitors were ushered in to the Viceregal presence.

That same afternoon, Hugh Merton called at the hotel. As he held out his arms to her, Caroline went to him and, putting her face against his shoulder, cried like a child. Hugh was her beloved father's friend and seemed now like a surrogate father.

'There, there, child,' he soothed, fully understanding her outburst. 'I am here, and you can tell me all your troubles. But don't cry, lass, I never could take a woman's tears!'

Caroline laughed and stood back. 'Oh Uncle Hugh! I am so glad to see you!'

'And I to see you, Caroline!' Merton replied gravely, remembering the girl he had seen five years ago, dressed in the latest fashion, a lady of leisure. He noted her thinner face, the slightly tanned skin and the hair dressed in a demure style. Yet for all this he found her more interesting now than the happy carefree girl he had known in London. She had gained in maturity and had conquered both sorrow and misfortune. Caroline also remembered the happier days in London.

'I have come to take you to my house. You shall stay with us while you are here,' Merton said.

'I shall like that very much, Uncle Hugh!'

'The family is most anxious to see you again.'

Richard and Chunilal stayed on at the Great Eastern Hotel, while Caroline went with her two maidservants to the Merton house in elegant Middleton Row, across the *maidan*.

Sybil Merton was standing on the veranda of her colonial-style house to welcome Caroline. She was, like her husband, large and florid-complexioned, with no pretensions of belonging to either the nobility or the gentry. Hugh Merton had made his fortune in the East with hard work and initiative. They had become fond of their adopted country, where they lived far more comfortably than they could have done in their native Midlands. She kept a check on her children, who gave themselves airs and pretended to be what they were not.

The Merton daughters had always been awed by Caroline's breeding, her education and accomplishments since they had once visited her at the Emerson house in Bayswater. Now they found the roles reversed; for while they were young ladies of leisure, Caroline had become an impecunious governess. But once they saw her walk gracefully up to their veranda, her head held high, they realised that changed circumstances might have lessened the richness of her clothes but had not diminished her dignity.

Sybil Merton served the afternoon tiffin, which included sandwiches with fillings of chutney, a paste of coriander and mint leaves, lemon-juice and pepper. There were curried puffs, an Indian version of sausage rolls, and cakes filled with the exotic fruits and spices of the East. Then turbanned servants, padding barefoot on the parquet floors, took the plates away and brought in an aromatic tea grown in Darjeeling, in the foothills of the Himalayas.

'Tell us about your life in Vijaypur,' Mrs Merton coaxed Caroline when they had settled down on the high veranda in the evening. A few carriages rolled past on the quiet road as darkness fell.

Caroline told them about her duties and gave non-committal descriptions of the Maharaja and his family.

'And have you met the Resident?' Miss Lucy Merton asked archly.

Caroline hoped that no one would notice her flushed cheeks or hear her heart beating faster at the mention of him. 'Indeed I have,' she replied calmly.

'He is ever so nice!' put in Beryl, the youngest daughter.

'You made that very clear the last time he was here,' Cynthia, the second daughter, observed.

Beryl giggled. 'I think he liked me, too!'

Mrs Merton called them to order. Had she, like her eldest daughter, noticed Caroline's changed countenance?

'He is very dedicated to his work,' Caroline remarked.

'Ay!' Mrs Merton sighed. 'Such a pity he doesn't come out of his shell. I did try to interest him in my Lucy, but . . .'

'Mama!' Lucy shrieked. 'Please!'

'That's all right, love. Caroline is one of the family . . .'

Lucy got up. 'Don't listen to Mama, Caroline! She is for ever trying to find us husbands,' she cried in distress.

'Don't protest so much,' Cynthia told her elder sister.

'Mama, why don't you try to interest him in me?' fifteen-year-old Beryl asked.

Mrs Merton laughed and ruffled her daughters' ringlets.

'Get on with you, young hussy. Have you no delicacy?'

'None!' Beryl announced joyously.

'He is cold and uncommunicative,' Lucy declared, 'and I do not wish to marry him.'

'Well, he is not offering for any of us,' Cynthia said matter-of-factly. 'So let us not take the trouble to reject him.'

Unaccountably, Caroline felt glad. They soon abandoned the subject of Julian Lindsay and matrimony as Lucy began to plan their programme for the next few days. 'You must get proper clothes for the tropics,' Cynthia observed. 'Your heavy English clothes won't do, once the hot weather starts.'

'You should really have a new wardrobe,' Lucy advised airily, fully aware that Caroline did not have the means to order an entire new wardrobe.

Caroline sensed the purpose of her remark, and replied quietly, 'Lucy, I should love a new wardrobe, but I can spend only what I have saved from two months' salary. Would that be enough, do you think, for a large number of dresses?'

Lucy was abashed. Mrs Merton tried to make amends for her daughter's lack of delicacy. 'We shan't shop at the big stores, dear. I know a tailor, Abdul Salim, who will make whatever you wish. He comes and sits on the veranda, so you can keep an eye on the work.'

The Merton girls and Caroline spent several days purchasing yards of various materials for the latter's gowns. The patient and skilful fingers of Abdul Salim fashioned a small but elegant wardrobe for Caroline. It was a far cry from the dresses designed by Monsieur Worth with his ruffles and ruches, but in the heat of India's climate the pastel muslins, soft cambric and light silk dresses with short sleeves and wide necklines were more suitable.

The sisters spent several pleasant days driving around in a barouche showing Caroline the sights of the new capital; wide Park Street with elegant apartments and offices, the cluster of shops in the Esplanade, Court House Road and the law courts, Camac Street with its stately mansions. They saw Fort William, the new arsenal of eastern India, and the Botanical Gardens, begun by Colonel Kyd, and the Eden Gardens financed and inspired by Emily Eden, the sister of the Governor-General, Lord Auckland.

The drives round Calcutta convinced Caroline that it was a city made in the image of Regency England with bits of baroque thrown in. She felt it had an Imperial grandeur suited to its role as the nerve centre of Britain's eastern domains.

One day they went up the slender minaret called the Ochterlony Monument from whose top they could see the city spread before them: the stylish British area, the sprawling and picturesque Bengali quarters with ornate houses, ships in full sail on the Hooghly, and verdant splashes at Garden Reach where the wealthy Europeans and Indians had 'country houses' for the summer months. The girls took Caroline and Richard to play croquet at the Tollygunge Club, a marshy area built up by one Major Tolly, and also to see the new Calcutta Rowing Club on the Dhakuria Lake. On Sundays they worshipped at the Gothic-style St Paul's Cathedral on the *maidan* or in old St John's Church, where Job Charnock was buried.

Richard always dropped in at the Mertons' in the late afternoon, and was always asked to stay to dinner. The evenings were cheerful and noisy affairs. Lucy sat on a chair gazing at the young Englishman, while Cynthia thumped on the piano, and Beryl sang off key. After dinner Lucy managed to take Richard to the walled-in garden. Caroline found all this diverting, feeling sorry for the pretty but insipid Lucy, who was not to know that Richard was infatuated with an exotic princess.

One evening Richard burst in at the Merton home, his eyes glittering with excitement. 'Oh, Caroline!' he cried, swinging her into an impromptu dance before Lucy's raised eyebrows. 'Something wonderful has happened!'

'Tell me,' Caroline said, laughing and releasing herself from his encircling arms.

'I have been offered a place in the Viceroy's personal

establishment! He was most impressed with my know-ledge of Indian history and languages!'

Caroline's eyes searched Richard's joyous face. 'Does this mean that you will not be returning to Vijaypur?' she asked quietly.

Richard looked speculatively at his friend, his blue eyes twinkling. 'It means a lot of things, Caroline,' he said softly. 'But of course I will go back to Vijaypur for a while . . .'

'I see,' she slowly replied.

Lucy heard the murmured words and leaped to the conclusion that Caroline and Richard had some sort of understanding. She rose from the settee where she had been watching the two talking. 'Mr Brooke, may I say how delighted I am?' she said stiffly, barely bothering to hide her disappointment.

'Thank you, Miss Merton,' he replied with a mischievous smile, his eyes still on the pensive Caroline.

'We must have a party to celebrate,' Lucy announced.

'We are going to a party at Government House the day after tomorrow,' Richard replied.

'We?' Lucy asked.

'You, Cynthia, your parents, of course, Caroline and I.'

'Oh, how divine!' Lucy exclaimed.

'Not really. The Vicereine is having a little party for some visitors from London.' Richard turned to Caroline. 'Does Lady Lawrence know you, by any chance?'

Caroline shook her head, perplexed. 'I have never met her.'

'Well, she asked after you.'

'That is very strange!'

'I think Julian must have requested her to ask you.'

'That was good of him.'

'Anyway, I told the Vicereine that you were staying with the Mertons. Perhaps that is why she decided to ask you all.'

'Oh, how marvellous! I must tell mama!' Lucy cried, and ran to inform the ladies.

Richard still had that enigmatic smile on his face. 'Well, dear girl, prepare to dazzle everyone at Government House,' he said. Caroline was puzzled by his new ebullience and nonchalance, but did not question him further.

The Merton ladies were excited on the morning of the Viceroy's dinner party. After an early luncheon of mutton vindaloo and biriyani, they all retired for a siesta to look their best for the evening.

CHAPTER
EIGHT

It was a warm evening. They went in two carriages: Mr
and Mrs Merton along with Richard were in one; Caroline, Lucy and Cynthia in the other. They drove to Court
House Road and turned into the drive of Government
House with its imposing classical façade. At the massive
portico, liveried servants helped them to alight. The
party then assembled and walked slowly through a
corridor lined with portraits of the men who had founded British India and up a broad flight of carpeted stairs to
the drawing-room used by the Viceroy when he entertained.

The room was in Regency style with apple-green walls
and ivory white doors and panels. The furniture was also
of that period: light and graceful and upholstered in pale
green and lilac. The Aubusson carpet was in the same
colours, while a large chandelier illuminated the scene.
The décor recreated the atmosphere of a Regency drawing-room, without any hint of the Indian ambience
except for the profusion of tuberoses and exotic orchids
that filled the room. It was very different from the
comfortable Dutch-colonial-style house of the Mertons,
where Hepplewhite furniture jostled with home-made
teakwood cabinets.

A richly dressed Indian major-domo announced their
names in a stentorian tone. Mrs Merton, wearing a

rose-coloured satin dress and glittering with rubies,
entered on the arm of her husband. Then followed
Richard Brooke. After him came the three young ladies.
Lucy invited one's attention at first glance—fair and
flushed, wearing a blue silk dress which flattered her
colouring. Cynthia was in pale blue, happy to let her
sister take the limelight. Yet it was Caroline who captured the admiration of the other guests. She wore a
cream silk dress with tiny puffed sleeves, simple unadorned bodice and a full billowing skirt embroidered
with green flowers. A double string of lustrous pearls
encircled her slender neck and merged with the creamy
glow of her shoulders.

Lady Lawrence greeted the newcomers in order of
precedence, but returned to Caroline to say, 'I have
been looking forward to meeting you, Miss Emerson.'

'It is gracious of you to invite me, your ladyship.'

Lady Lawrence smiled. 'Well, I certainly would have
invited you on my own, as Sir Julian Lindsay asked me to
meet you, but dear Edward was urging me to do so as
well.'

Caroline felt her blood turn to water. Her wide eyes
expressed her confusion.

Lady Lawrence enquired, 'You do know the Honourable Edward Lockwood? He said he had met you in
London.' She turned to summon someone with a wave
of her silk and sandalwood fan.

Caroline looked past her to the man who was crossing
the room towards them. He came and took her hand,
and kissed it.

'How are you, Caroline?' Edward Lockwood
murmured.

Caroline was speechless as she stared at him.

'Dear Caroline, how good to see you!' he murmured

again, hoping to thaw her.

'What brings you to India?' Caroline asked coldly.

Lady Lawrence's eyebrows rose a fraction at this singular greeting. Then her thin lips twitched with a smile of understanding. 'I shall leave you both to get acquainted again,' she said, and returned to her other guests.

'That was hardly an affectionate greeting, Caro, especially after the trouble I took to meet you,' Edward said affably.

'Why did you bother?'

Edward cocked his handsome head to one side, as if to ascertain her attitude more clearly. 'I was sent to Egypt on some work . . . so I travelled further east, as I had a sudden desire to see you. Your Aunt Hester told me how you had buried yourself in some godforsaken place as governess to the brats of an oriental potentate.'

Caroline found herself looking at the young man in wonder. 'Could this be the man I once loved?' She shook her head. 'No, it was not love,' she thought with a surge of gladness. 'If it had been love, I would not find him so absurd now.'

'Why are you smiling?' he asked, irritated by the irony of her expression.

'No special reason,' she said in a gentler tone. 'Come now, Edward, let us sit down. Everyone is wondering why we are glaring at each other like prize-fighters.'

He led her to a sofa, watched intently by Lady Lawrence and the Mertons. Caroline found herself talking politely to Edward, who was surprised by her impersonal courtesy. He had expected a dramatic, even turbulent, reunion, but had not envisaged something so casual and banal as sitting together and talking of London and their common acquaintances. He felt utterly deflated. Had he tormented himself with guilt and remorse for nothing? She did not even seem to remember their past relationship.

After about twenty minutes, Caroline rose and beckoned to Lucy. Turning to the frowning Edward, she murmured, 'I want you to meet Miss Lucy Merton. You should find a great deal in common.'

Lucy gazed up at the young aristocrat with an adoring expression as Caroline introduced them and then walked away to join the group round Lady Lawrence.

The Vicereine managed to combine the qualities of an artistocrat and pioneer with grace and wit. She had lived in India through the stormy years of the Mutiny and suffered the ordeals with her husband and his brother Henry, who had died during the siege of Lucknow. Neither embittered nor intimidated, this spirited English lady had learnt to understand the country loved by her husband.

Hearing her talk knowledgeably about Indian problems, whether they pertained to politics or the availability of certain fruits, Caroline realised why the Resident had wanted her to meet Lady Lawrence.

There were other interesting guests: a senior army officer from the North-West Frontier, who described the depredations of the frontier tribesmen in the Punjab; a former official of the East India Company who had assumed the airs of a nobleman after despoiling the country for many years; an intense Oriental scholar keen to find the clue to the ancient Brahmin script; a Presbyterian missionary and his wife eager to proseletyse.

With all of them the Viceroy and Vicereine talked with interest and warmth, genuinely eager to know of their work and problems, and offered advice with a tact and firmness that Caroline could not but admire. To her,

Lady Lawrence was kindness itself, advising her on matters of dress, food and behaviour with a maternal attitude. She expressed her approval that Caroline had read widely about Indian culture and customs.

'What a pity it would be if you were to leave India so soon after taking the trouble to acquaint yourself with the country,' Lady Lawrence observed, smiling in the direction of the Honourable Edward Lockwood.

'I have no intention of leaving in the near future, your ladyship,' Caroline replied warmly.

The Vicereine glanced at Edward, wondering how he would react. The young man smiled indulgently at them both before returning his attention to Lucy Merton.

Dinner was served with considerable style and ceremony in a vast dining-room, once more recreated to evoke the English décor of the 1770s when Warren Hastings, the Governor-General, and his German wife Maria set the fashion at Government House. Lady Lawrence, though, had brought to the imposing room her own preference for light colours and designs. The food served, however, was heavy and the courses interminable, and not at all suited to the sultry heat of a Calcutta summer. Nevertheless Caroline was delighted to savour the forgotten taste of English cooking after so many months.

The party ended early, as the Lawrences liked to read before bed. As they parted, Edward told Caroline that he hoped to meet her again.

Caroline ensured that she was not his only guest when Edward invited her to see an English play at the Minerva Theatre in the British area. The theatre was built as a replica of any of its kind in London, with plush seats, red velvet draperies and a generous use of gilt. The high ceiling saved the hall from being unbearably hot, though ladies resorted to a liberal use of silk fans. During the interval, attendants brought in trays of iced drinks and cakes for the audience.

This was the first opportunity Caroline had had to see how Indians responded to western culture. She was pleasantly surprised to find a large number of educated Indians in the audience who seemed to show a keener appreciation of Hamlet's dilemmas than the British army officers and merchants who sat in the balcony.

'I now want to see a Bengali play,' she announced when they returned to the Mertons' house.

'Don't be absurd!' the Honourable Edward Lockwood exclaimed, 'What would you do there?'

'Why, see the play, of course!' Caroline retorted. 'I can understand a little Bengali. It is not very different from Hindi.'

'You mean to tell me you actually speak the local language?' Edward queried. 'Why, when English can be used?'

'That is a question you must ask His Excellency the Resident of Vijaypur, for it was Sir Julian who advised me to learn Hindi. He speaks it fluently. I believe he knows Bengali as well.'

Edward stared at the girl. 'My poor Caro!' he said softly. 'What sort of people do you work with?'

'A very unusual sort,' she replied, a slow colour staining her cheeks.

'I can see that,' he muttered, his eyes on Caroline's face.

Richard smiled ironically at the young aristocrat. 'Yes,' he agreed. 'Our Resident is an unusual man—respected by both the Indians and the British.'

'Sounds odd to me,' Edward said peevishly.

Caroline felt her temper rising. 'As I was saying, Uncle Hugh. Could I see a Bengali play?' she asked calmly.

Hugh Merton glanced round the table, a slight twitching of his lips betraying his amusement. Depending so greatly on the Viceroy's goodwill, he dared not offend Sir John's young guest from England, yet he had no intention of dampening Caroline's enthusiasm.

'Why, of course, my dear. It shall be arranged. We shall all make up a party to see one of dramas based on the epics. I think they're doing *The Abduction of Sita* now in a Bengali theatre in north Calcutta.'

'Splendid!' Caroline enthused. 'Let us go!'

'You can count me out,' Edward said stiffly.

'Oh, but Mr Lockwood!' Cynthia protested. 'It will be a treat. You will love the theatrical effects!'

'I would much prefer to spend my time at Government House,' he replied with icy disdain.

'That is perfectly all right,' Caroline rejoined. 'We shall go without you.'

The next day Caroline was accompanied by all the Mertons (except Lucy who, professed the same reluctance as Edward) and Richard to the Bengali play. The theatre was larger and more garishly decorated than the Minerva, and the ancient story held Caroline's attention until the end. Equally interesting was the audience, composed of Bengalis of all social strata, who constantly interrupted the performance with impassioned pleas to the unfortunate Princess Sita to resist her abductor and remember her beloved Rama.

'The Ramayana story is similar to that of the Iliad,' Caroline observed on the way home.

'There is a theory,' Richard told her, 'that the Indian epic Ramayana and the Greek Iliad are drawn from a common folklore of the central Asian peoples. Scholars are working on linguistic evidence to prove it.'

'I wish I could spend my time digging into the past,' she said wistfully.

'Why don't you?'

Caroline sighed. 'Oh, I could have done that if I was a lady of leisure. But, like you, I have to earn my living.'

'You need not, you know. Not any more,' Richard said cryptically. 'You have other choices.'

Caroline shook her head. 'No, Richard, I have none.'

'Are you certain? Don't pursue a mirage, Caroline. There can be nothing but pain in that. Believe me.'

Caroline felt her spirits darkening. 'I believe you,' she said quietly.

To appease the Honourable Edward, Mrs Merton proposed a day's picnic at their country house at Garden Reach, where the waters of the River Hooghly almost lapped the thick green lawns.

They set out in several carriages, travelling through the elegant westernised areas of Calcutta, past the Bengali sections with ornate houses, sprawling gardens and temples, and then on the narrow rural highway along the banks of the river, until they came to Merton's Folly. It was a small but picturesque villa, set in lush surroundings, designed as a rural retreat from the bustle of Calcutta.

Caroline went to the river, her crisp muslin crinoline billowing in the fresh breeze, a broad-brimmed hat shading her face. Cynthia and Beryl followed her, but Richard hung back with Lucy, who was holding a silk parasol over her golden head, determined to avoid getting tanned and freckled as Caroline showed signs of doing.

Eager to make up for his earlier peevishness, Edward joined Caroline and was always at her side, talking and laughing. She fell into the easy mood produced, she felt, by the soft and soporific air of Bengal. He walked arm-in-arm with her through mango groves whose unfurling blossoms drew a cluster of bees. The sharp scent of mango blossoms mingling with the warm spring air and the river breeze made Caroline feel a little dizzy. She sat on one of the wicker chairs suspended from a tall banyan tree, swinging gently to and fro. The river flowed past, carrying narrow boats laden with wares, and in the deeper waters were larger barges taking jute and tea to the sea-going ships at Diamond Harbour.

The boatman sang mournful, tender hymns to the eternal river, which stirred Caroline strangely. Sensing that Edward wished to talk to Caroline, Cynthia and Beryl left them alone.

Edward stood beside Caroline on the springy grass. 'Don't you feel you've strayed into some jungle paradise?' he asked.

'Paradise?' she said, head bent to one side to catch the cool river breeze.

'Yes, paradise,' he insisted. 'All this lush flora and fauna belongs there. Anyway, it's a far cry from London.'

'Yes,' she agreed, 'that is indisputable.'

Edward suddenly knelt on the grass and clasped Caroline's hand in both of his. 'Don't you miss England, Caroline?' he asked intently, solemn grey eyes searching sparkling green ones. Then inexplicably he saw that her eyes had become veiled by some inscrutable expression. 'Well, Caroline? Don't you?'

Caroline swung herself on the wicker chair, accompanied by sounds of a creaking branch and rustle of leaves overhead as a young monkey frolicked. Parrots and koels screamed in protest at his antics. 'Sometimes,' she said softly. 'But it's a life I have left behind, Edward.'

'You can return to it—if you choose,' he said clearly.

Their eyes again considered each other. As Edward rose to stand by her, to elaborate, a flurry of leaves and feathers cascaded over them, followed by the noisy descent of the young monkey, who had been slapped by his mother for his misdemeanours. Adding to this existing cacaphony was Beryl's loud lament on the ordeals of her favourite parrots nesting on the banyan tree.

Caroline laughed and slid off the swing, straining her eyes to look up at the ruffled feathers of Beryl's parrots. Beryl picked up her skirts and pursued the monkey, abusing it in Bengali.

Edward looked as ruffled as the parrots, and sighed in exasperation. 'I spoke too soon. This is no paradise. It's a blasted market-place! As for the Merton girls, I do wish they were more sedate!'

Again Caroline laughed, more at Edward's annoyance than at Beryl's antics. 'I think they are charming girls—especially Lucy,' she said archly, glancing at the eldest Miss Merton who sat demurely on the wide circular veranda while a Bengali maid fanned her with a large palmyra leaf. He followed her gaze and shrugged.

Beryl returned, flushed and moist-faced after chasing the monkey off to the riverside. 'Here,' she said, handing two glasses of coconut water to her guests. 'This will restore you for the walk back to the house. Lunch is ready.'

As they walked back, they stopped to call Richard and

Cynthia, who were sitting by the water's edge, deep in discussion.

After luncheon, Mrs Merton segregated her guests. While her daughters and Caroline retreated to a large day-room for a siesta, Edward and Richard sat smoking on the shady veranda. Caroline heard their murmured conversation and tossed in bed, troubled by Edward's suggestions. When finally she got up to have a drink of water, she found Cynthia looking at her with a happy smile.

'Life is full of unexpected meetings, isn't it?' Cynthia asked, blue eyes dreamy.

Caroline nodded and watched her intently. Then she lay down again and thought that, whatever Padmini might feel, the Resident at any rate would be glad to know of Richard's new friend. Abruptly she sat up again. 'Julian Lindsay!' she almost said aloud. 'Am I still thinking of him? How foolish of me, when Edward has come so far to see me!'

With this thought, she drifted into a deep sleep, induced this time by the heavily spiced luncheon and the soft river air.

On the long drive back to Middleton Row, Lucy joined Caroline in the open curricle, causing the Honourable Edward Lockwood to frown. Cynthia, Beryl and Richard flew past in a high phaeton, while the older Mertons followed slowly in a barouche. Caroline kept up a steady conversation to alleviate Edward's annoyance and Lucy's gloom.

Caroline spent the next few days exploring other parts of the city, accompanied by Richard, who was as interested as she was to discover Calcutta. They went to the Imperial Library to browse through books and historical documents, making notes on matters that took their fancy. Temples along the river-bank beckoned to them, and there they watched from a distance the rich and elaborate ceremonies of worship. At their request, Mr Merton took them with him to Diamond Harbour, where his ship waited to carry cheap cotton, jute and tea to England.

Now, Caroline was beginning to understand how the lure of commerce had impelled Europeans to travel over many seas to grasp the opportunities for trade, and why soldiers and administrators had come in the wake of the merchants to safeguard British interests.

In the days that followed, Edward could not, despite every ploy, talk undisturbed to Caroline. Every time he visited the Merton house either Lucy or Beryl would join them. (Cynthia was usually busy pointing out rare species of flowers to Richard in the garden.) What exasperated him was that Caroline, far from resenting the intrusions, welcomed them. It was as though she were afraid to be alone with him.

Indeed Caroline was determined not to be alone with Edward. She was afraid of falling once more under the spell of his grey eyes and the easy-going charm which had captivated her in London two years ago. Yet, as she stole glances at him, Caroline found that Edward stood in far greater danger of being captivated by her. Gone was the lightness from his face as his eyes followed her round, as he listened eagerly to her descriptions of Vijaypur.

'You have changed, Caroline,' he told her on the eve of her departure.

'In what way, Edward?'

He shrugged his shoulders. 'It's difficult to explain . . . but I can see the change,' he said quietly.

'I've had time to grow up since papa's death,' Caroline

replied calmly, remembering the autumn afternoon when Edward's evasive letter reached her, and the wound it had inflicted on her and her father.

Edward also remembered his letter; for a moment his handsome face darkened in remorse. 'Let me write to you, Caro,' he said softly. 'I'll explain everything and then perhaps we might . . . take up where we left off.'

Caroline's eyes widened in disbelief. Then she nodded and said with composure. 'I should be happy to hear from you, Edward.'

He bent his head to hers, but she drew back, without knowing why, and instead gave him her hand in a cordial manner.

That night Caroline lay sleepless on the high brass bed, wondering whether she could go back to the life she had left behind.

'What would it be like to be Edward Lockwood's wife?' she thought as she stared out of the high windows into the dark, flower-scented night. 'I need not work, any more. Neither need I occupy a subservient role in Society.' She thought of the condescending manner in which Mrs Dalrymple had treated her in Vijaypur, and wondered how they would react if she returned there as the Honourable Mrs Edward Lockwood, sister-in-law to the Earl of Elverston? 'Would it not be lovely to return to England, secure in my position as Edward's wife?'

Unaccountably the prospect failed to excite her. 'Ah well,' she consoled herself. 'He has not made any proposal. Once I am back in Vijaypur, we shall again go our separate ways.'

CHAPTER
NINE

DURING THE long journey back to Vijaypur, Caroline was quiet, deep in thoughts of the past and present. In Calcutta, the past had caught up with her, had tried to intrude into the present and influence the future, but she wanted the future to be separate from the past. She wondered how in the end the two would be reconciled. She found herself wondering if Edward Lockwood had really come to seek her in India or had it been a chance encounter? If so, why was he anxious to revive the forgotten relationship?

Richard spoke more often, but he too fell into sudden silences. Caroline realised that he had come to the threshold of a decisive action and left him alone to sort out his ideas.

After five days they were back in Jaipur, where the carriages from Vijaypur were there to meet them outside the railway station. Chunilal supervised all the arrangements. They had a light breakfast in the quiet, clean Railway Rest Rooms and then set off for Vijaypur.

In the month that they had been away, the brief spring of north India had come and gone. It was early April, and though the wind was cool, especially in the wooded hills through which they passed, the sun was strong. The jacarandas were gone but the mango blossoms sent out an exotic fragrance. The rich profusion of flowers was gone as well.

Caroline felt a sense of homecoming as the carriage crossed the border of Vijaypur state. The high arched gate dating from the eleventh century still stood proudly, flying the Maharaja's colours. Here the Afghans from Ghori and Ghazni had been met by Vijaypuri warriors, slain and scattered, before the invaders rushed into the more fertile Gangetic plains. The fields were ablaze with golden stalks of *bajra* and other millets, the hardy crops suited to the thin sandy soil of Rajputana. She saw women in their voluminous skirts and veils tending the fields with their menfolk, while others brought in water on enormous pitchers from near-by water holes.

They rode past the town of Vijaypur with its narrow streets, crowded shops displaying everything from the coiled *jelabi* sweetmeat to sparkling jewels. Cows were few, and fitted with bells on their horns as they meandered through the narrow lanes, while stately camels with supercilious expressions carrying burdens swayed past everyone. They were the darlings of the desert and more sacred than cows. Caroline had come now and then into town to buy lace or ribbons, or tinkling glass bangles for Pannabai and Chunibai. The townsfolk knew her as 'Teacher mem-saheb', while Richard was 'Master saheb'.

Leaving the town behind, the carriages took the broad avenue which led to the Maharaja's palace. Caroline leaned out of the window to see it in its luminous glory with its round arches, porticoes, pillars, round turrets and towers. It did not have the grandeur of buildings in Calcutta or the lightness of Muslim architecture. The Rajput style was different: lavish but not light, decorative but durable. The palace stood between Devgiri

Hill and Lake Rashmi, which glittered in the brilliant afternoon sunshine.

Retainers rushed out to open the carriages doors and carry their luggage inside. Within a short while, Caroline was back in her rooms getting ready for a bath, while Pannabai and her niece unpacked her clothes. For dinner she chose a peacock-blue silk dress made in Calcutta in accordance with the latest vogue in London, with an enormous billowing crinoline, pinched-in waist, wide but shallow neckline and puffed short sleeves. Her maid-servant had remembered to put the small wreath of camellias over Caroline's hair, which was loosely knotted at the nape of her neck, the way she had seen Bengali women do it in Calcutta. The Maharani sent a note asking Caroline to come to her apartment for dinner.

Caroline entered Sitadevi's suite and sank into a deep curtsy before her. 'Miss Caroline, how happy I am to see you,' Sitadevi declared as she took her unadorned hands in her bejewelled ones.

'And I, Your Highness, am happy to be back,' she replied, and then curtsied to the Crown Prince and the Resident. Princess Padmini rose from a chair and embraced her. 'I have missed you,' she said in a tight, sad voice. Alarmed, Caroline glanced at Lindsay, who was standing with Prince Kamal. His expression as usual was remote, betraying nothing. She looked away.

They sat down on the low brocade sofas favoured by Sitadevi, and on the low carved tables were jasmine and tuberoses in silver bowls. The windows were open to let in the evening breeze. Several attendants entered bearing trays of sherbet. As a sign of respect, neither the Resident nor Prince Kamal drank alcohol before the chief Maharani.

'Perhaps you had better tell Miss Caroline all about the wedding,' Padmini said, looking at the grave-faced Resident. 'She should know.'

Caroline felt a coldness creep into her heart, especially when she saw Lindsay. Was he getting married? Is that why he looked so withdrawn? She sat down next to the Princess, and with an air of assumed indifference asked, 'What wedding?'

The Resident put down his glass and glanced at the Maharani, who nodded with a smile. 'Miss Emerson, you will be happy to know that a marriage had been arranged between Prince Kamal and Princess Indumati of Tewar.'

Caroline felt absurdly relieved to hear that it was only the Crown Prince who was getting married. She rose, and extended her hand in congratulations.

'I do believe you have brought us good fortune, Miss Emerson,' the Prince said with unaccustomed seriousness.

Lindsay sat looking exultant. 'This marriage will strengthen the Crown Prince's position. The Maharaja of Tewar has much influence among the Rajputs. Pran Singh will not find it so easy to stir up trouble,' he stated.

'I am glad for His Highness,' Caroline said cheerfully, wondering whether Prince Kamal regarded his own marriage in the same cold light as had the Resident.

'I knew you would be,' said Sitadevi. 'You have been a friend to my daughter. So you will also be glad to know that Padmini, too, will marry soon.'

Instinctively Caroline turned to the Princess, who sat motionless staring dully out of the window.

'Tell my friend and teacher your plans for me, Sir Julian.' Her voice was cold.

Lindsay inclined his head in mock obedience. 'As you

command, Princess,' he said lightly, and then turned to Caroline. 'The Maharaja of Tewar has a younger brother who is still unmarried. Strangely enough he never married because his horoscope also is unsuitable for matrimony. Now it appears that two such inauspicious combinations cancel each other. So when we were in Tewar two weeks ago to finalise our Prince's betrothal, I made a suggestion to the Maharaja about his younger brother Prince Uday. It was favourably received. We hope to settle the matter at the time of Prince Kamal's wedding. Prince Uday Singh will naturally wish to see his future bride.'

Caroline looked at Padmini, who heard all this with little emotion. 'I hope . . . you are happy, Princess,' she murmured.

The Princess shrugged her shoulders. 'Happy? To marry an old man nearing forty? My brother's uncle-in-law?' she asked derisively, and then, addressing her brother, said, 'Do you realise that if I marry Uday Singh, I shall be your aunt, and that you will have to touch my feet in homage?' She laughed mirthlessly. The Prince bent his head, but the Maharani said gently, 'You will be safe in Tewar. Here I always worry about you.'

Padmini seemed to be indifferent; she had obviously accepted the idea, as there was no alternative. 'Sir Julian is happy,' she said bitterly. 'He believes in marriages of convenience.'

Caroline stared at the patterns on the Persian carpet, lost in thought.

'One day, Princess, you will thank me,' the Resident said calmly.

'Shall I?' Padmini asked tearfully. 'I wonder!'

Caroline raised her eyes and found Lindsay regarding her thoughtfully. 'What do you think, Miss Emerson?'

'Of Padmini's future? Who can say, Your Excellency? Aren't these matters decided by fate?'

'Ah, now you are beginning to sound like an oriental!' he observed.

Caroline did not reply at once. He had already expressed his views on the folly of romance and the wisdom of arranged marriages. Yet she could not let this opportunity pass without expressing her view.

'It is a pity that the Rajputs no longer follow the ancient system of *swayamvara*,' she said with trepidation.

Lindsay and the others looked at her, surprised that she knew of the custom whereby a girl chose her husband from the assembled suitors.

'Who told you of this?' the Resident asked, curious.

'I saw a play in Calcutta—a Bengali play—where they referred to Sita's *swayamvara*. It seems that the ancient Indians allowed a woman to choose her own husband. And marriages from such arrangements turned out to be happy.' Caroline paused to see how far she had irritated him. She was surprised instead by the expression of warm approval on his face.

'I believe they were, Miss Emerson,' Lindsay said gently. 'But the princesses in those days did not create sensations by trying to defy their established traditions.' He glanced at Padmini, who sat still like a statue, tearful and bitter.

The conversation reverted to Calcutta. Prompted by the Resident, Caroline told the others about her experiences there, and they listened with interest. Even Padmini abandoned her air of angry bitterness when Caroline described her visit to the Bengali theatre, the busy Diamond Harbour where Hugh Merton transacted business, and the Dakshineshwar temple where

Hindus flocked in thousands to meet and hear Rama-krishna.

'This saintly man has immense powers,' Caroline said with awe. 'Powers that cannot be explained by physical laws. It is said that people are transformed by meeting him.'

'Did you meet him?' Lindsay asked, intrigued.

'No, the crowd was too thick, but we saw him, and when his gaze met ours we felt . . . moved . . .' she replied in a hushed tone.

'I have heard his name,' Sitadevi observed. 'He is a great man . . . But I cannot imagine how you came to hear of him.'

'People talked about him even at Government House. I felt I just had to see him.'

'India has always produced such men,' the Resident said, gazing out of the window into the warm April night. 'They seem to come whenever they are needed.' He looked at Caroline with a strange intensity. 'I must say, Miss Emerson, that I did not expect you to become interested in this aspect of Indian life.'

'Every aspect of Indian life interests me, especially those which are unfamiliar,' Caroline remarked. 'They open up a whole new world of ideas and experiences.'

He regarded Caroline with an expression that quick-ened her pulse. 'Can it be that he really approves?' she asked herself. 'For once, he is satisfied to listen, and does not wish to contradict me.'

Indeed for the rest of the evening the Resident was quiet, almost preoccupied, with thoughts of his own. He listened as Caroline continued her account of what she had seen in Calcutta, but did not question her as he had earlier in the evening. Sitadevi and her children eagerly asked her about many things: particularly about the

Viceroy, Sir John Lawrence, who was antagonistic towards Maharaja Kedar Singh. They noticed that Caroline became reticent, almost wary, when describing Government House and its inhabitants. Neither was Lindsay unaware of her guarded manner, and he wondered what had happened there to make Caroline loath to reveal too much.

After dinner in the Maharani's apartment, the Prince took leave of his mother, and the Princess also left in haste for her own rooms. Caroline and Lindsay thanked Sitadevi and walked slowly along the lamp-lit corridor cooled by the night wind. Outside in the gardens, a waxing moon lit up the unfurling scarlet blossoms of the Flame of the Forest trees.

The Resident halted by a high open window, and stared intently at Caroline. She stood facing him, wondering why he had stopped. 'Has he something important to tell me?' she asked herself.

'I am glad you went to Calcutta, Miss Emerson,' he said quietly. 'You seem to have acquainted yourself with many aspects of India not known to you before.'

'Yes,' Caroline replied. 'There is more to see and learn there than in the confines of a palace!'

His eyebrows rose in a query. 'Does Vijaypur bore you then, Miss Emerson?' Before she could reply, he sighed. 'I suppose it can be tedious for a young lady accustomed to travel, society and entertainment.'

'No, Sir Julian,' she hastened to contradict him. 'I am never bored here . . . not when you . . .' she faltered, colouring.

He looked at her with a new interest. Seeing the slight smile on his face, Caroline resumed soberly, 'You have told me that I can help you . . . to lighten your burden . . . I am trying to do that. Besides, I like teaching the princesses. They are such lovely girls.'

The Resident nodded. 'I am glad, Miss Emerson, that you feel this way. The fact that you want to understand them and appreciate their traditions makes it easier for all of us. It is not something I ever expected when you came here three months ago.' He paused, and rested his keen gaze on her. 'In fact, things which are wearisome to some western women never seem to tire you. When you described Calcutta and your journeys, it was as though you found every novelty exciting, every discomfort a challenge.'

The girl glowed at his praise. She felt a sweet warmth flooding her and would have liked just then to melt into his arms. Yet a vigilant instinct warned her to remain cool.

'Then your fear that I would treat my sojourn here as a holiday and an adventure was unfounded?' she asked airily.

'Quite unfounded, Miss Emerson,' he said in a low voice filled with laughter. 'I even wonder if I have not met a kindred spirit in you.'

They gazed at each other, endless questions pursuing each other until Caroline drew back, aware of the peril of surrendering to his magnetism. She knew him to change from ardour to aloofness without warning, and resolved never to suffer the misery that came in the wake of those changes.

'I am glad you find me so, Sir Julian. From you it is lofty praise indeed, since you have a high opinion of yourself. But I wonder if the tribute is justified? I continue to harbour different views from you on many matters.' She spoke hurriedly and in some agitation.

'Such as?' he asked, a trifle amused by her asperity.

'Such as an arranged marriage for Princess Padmini.

Did you observe her misery when you announced the news to me?'

The Resident's smile faded, but the softness in his eyes remained, adding to Caroline's unease and confusion.

'Miss Emerson,' he said gently. 'Can we not remember the many ideas we share rather than this one matter where we differ and where I know, because of my wider experience, that I am doing the correct thing?'

'If you wish it,' she replied, surprised by his tone and manner. Where had his hauteur and intolerance gone?

'I do,' he replied, and took both her hands in his. He held them for a moment and then slowly released them. 'Good night, Miss Emerson,' he murmured. 'I, too, am glad you are back.'

'Good night, Sir Julian,' Caroline said, and went towards the corridor that connected the Maharani's wing with her own.

It was a long time before she could compose herself to sleep. For hours, until dawn broke over Vijaypur, she kept seeing the tall and imperious figure of the Resident in the lamp-lit corridor, speaking to her in a manner he had never used before.

'Why am I letting my imagination run riot?' she chided herself. 'He has told me that I am open-minded and knowledgeable. Surely such approval does not mean anything more than just that?'

Nevertheless a stubborn joyous sensation within her could not be suppressed.

CHAPTER
TEN

CAROLINE FELL back into her old routine with a mixture of relief and restlessness. Teaching the princesses kept her mind occupied, giving her little time for introspection. Nevertheless the cause for restlessness was always there: the grave, attractive and enigmatic Resident who had once more retreated into his walled life after the friendly encounter in the corridor. She wondered if she had been wise in her cool attitude to Edward Lockwood. Richard Brooke's subtle advice was never far from her thoughts. 'And who knows Sir Julian Lindsay better than his young, admiring disciple from Derbyshire?' she thought. Had he implied that she should bestow more warmth on Edward?

In this mood of uncertainty Caroline went to the music-room late one afternoon when the princesses had departed after their lessons. She opened the grand piano and sat with her fingers poised over the ivory keys. After a moment she began to play a tune loved and remembered from her girlhood days. The limpid tender tones filled the room, mingling with the amber sunlight filtering through the latticed windows. The melody soothed and revived in her all her old dreams, as yet unfulfilled, but which she refused to abandon for reality. After finishing the piece, she paused before starting another.

'That was lovely,' a deep voice said. Caroline turned

and saw Lindsay sitting in an armchair near one of the windows.

'I didn't hear you come in,' Caroline exclaimed.

Lindsay regarded her gravely, almost as if he were going to ask her something, but suddenly changed his mind, and asked in a terse voice, 'Isn't that "The Maiden's Prayer"?' She nodded.

'Do all maidens have the same prayer?' Lindsay asked quietly. 'Or do some want power, some riches, some love . . .' He looked steadily at her, as if he knew more than he showed.

'I suppose so,' she replied in confusion, wondering why he was suddenly interested in her opinion. 'What else can I play for you, Sir Julian?' she asked abruptly to change the subject because she feared that, under the spell of music and his disturbing presence, she would end up by confessing her own prayers.

He sensed this at once, and said briskly, 'Actually, I came in here to ask if you would like to come for a ride with me to Devgiri Hill. I thought I would visit the palace up there to see if it can be used for housing the bridal party from Tewar.'

'How is that? I understood that the wedding would be held, as is the custom, in the bride's home?'

'That is so, but today I received a communication to say that there is an epidemic in the countryside round Tewar and they would prefer to have the wedding here.'

'That will mean a lot of work, won't it?'

'We'll manage, and you'll help, I hope.'

'Of course,' Caroline replied.

'Then would you like to come up to the hill with me?'

She closed the lid of the piano. 'I'll change, and join you in a minute.'

Devgiri Hill, looming like a huge shadow over the

palace, was surrounded by many legends. The oldest was that when the goddess Parvati slew a demon on the hill, the grateful king of that ancient time built a temple to commemorate her victory. Since then, it had been the place of worship of the Vijaypur rulers. The temple was built in a severe style out of the luminous greyish-pink stone found in the near-by quarries. The high, austere building contrasted with the light summer palace built by Ravi Singh, one of Kedar Singh's ancestors, not far from the temple, in imitation of the Taj Mahal. Though of Persian design, the place was called 'Mahadev Vilas'— 'The Abode of Mahadev', who was the consort of Parvati.

They rode across the palace grounds and out beyond the huge wrought-iron gates. The hill spread over half a mile and was about a thousand feet high, with a winding road leading to the top. At one spot, an earlier Maharaja had built a thousand and one steps up to the summit. Anyone who desperately wanted a boon from the mighty goddess would climb the steep steps, which led directly to the temple door. As they rode, Lindsay pointed out places of interest to Caroline: where a handful of Vijaypuri nobles had ambushed a Turkish army that had come to sack the sacred temple in the fourteenth century, or where a ruler had taken refuge among the wooded fastness after his defeat at the hands of a Moghul emperor.

'The Maharaja hid there for ten years, eating berries and fruits, rather than accept a suzerainty of the Moghuls, coming down only when the emperor had died and he could ride out at the head of his valiant warriors to harass the court of Delhi,' Lindsay told her.

'These hills remind me of Scotland.' Caroline observed. 'And the Rajputs with their fierce pride and sense of honour are not unlike the Scots.'

He smiled. 'That's why I like it here. My family is originally from Scotland, though after Culloden they moved south to Derbyshire.'

'I guessed as much,' Caroline replied gently. 'Strangely enough,' she continued in the same tone, 'I thought you were yet another member of the Maharaja's family when I first saw you. Of course the blue eyes were rather unusual, but I've seen them now and then among north Indians.'

'Yes, especially among the Pathans. Must be a legacy of Alexander's armies in Taxila,' Lindsay said with a smile. Then suddenly the smile vanished, and he remarked more quietly, 'I was saved during the Mutiny in a dangerous situation because I managed to escape disguised as a Pathan. Even my wife could not recognise me when I rushed home . . .'

He drew his horse to a sudden halt, himself amazed that for the first time in ten years he had spoken about a subject so painful. Caroline reined in her horse also, and looked at him with infinite sympathy, willing him to continue. As he gazed into her eyes, he saw not the usual defiant fires but a gentle glow, full of compassion and understanding.

Lindsay went on, driven by a need to tell her of that buried grief. 'Priscilla screamed, thinking I was a Pathan, and only when I spoke, and . . . took her in my arms . . . did she realise who I was. Then she began laughing, like an enormously amused child. It was then that I suggested that she should leave Calcutta by ship, disguised as an Indian girl. Of course it was more difficult with her fair colouring, but I thought it could be done. If we used henna on her hair and kohl around her eyes she could pass for a fair Hindu girl.'

'And did . . . Priscilla agree?' Caroline asked softly.

Lindsay let out a deep sigh and shook his head. 'No, she refused . . . She insisted that I accompany her, but I had to move with my soldiers to Meerut. So she stayed on, hiding in the house of a Bengali friend in Calcutta, who risked his own and his family's safety by sheltering her. It was a hot summer and she caught cholera and . . . was soon gone. British ships were lying at anchor just five miles away . . .' He gazed absently at the lake down below as though its glittering waters reminded him of the River Hooghly that flowed through Calcutta and could have taken Priscilla to safety.

The stricken look on his face touched Caroline deeply. She spoke to him gently. 'Some women, Sir Julian, cannot stand hardship. Some men cannot take heartache. Your wife . . . my father . . . they were the gentle, yet unbending kinds. We . . . you and I . . . are more resilient. Have you seen lotus stalks in ponds further east? How they suddenly bend under the weight of their beautiful proud heads? They're like your Priscilla and my father, while the humble reeds like me withstand storms and heat.'

The haunted look had gone from Lindsay's eyes, as he looked at her, while a smile lit their sapphire depths. 'Caroline,' he said softly. 'You're not a humble reed. You are like those fragrant yet resilient camellias in my garden that gladden the summer nights.'

Caroline felt as if she had floated away from her saddle to the dazzling gold spires of the hilltop temple.

Lindsay urged his horse to move closer to hers, and held out his hand. She took it with a sudden new shyness. 'Come, Caroline,' he said in a tone that made her heart turn over in her breast. 'Let's go up and see the palace above before it gets dark.'

They rode quickly and in silence for the remainder of the way, as the birds were flying back to their nests in the trees and the sun's rays slanted with the approaching twilight. Lindsay led the way through the clearings in the woods, taking the more gentle slopes. Soon they were there, and Caroline cried out in admiration when she dismounted and saw the palace. The city of Vijaypur lay beneath them, wrapped in a haze of amber light. The lake shone with the glitter of splintered glass, and Lotus Mahal floating on the molten gold water seemed like a huge iridescent pearl.

'It was worth the climb, wasn't it?' Lindsay asked with a wry smile, as he stood next to her on the terrace of Mahadev Vilas. Caroline nodded, turning to look at him and seeing in his eyes a message that made the years of sadness fall away from her.

'Well, Maharaja Ravi Singh certainly did something worth while when he built this palace, ruining the Vijaypur economy in the process,' he observed, his tone once more brisk and dry. He took her round the palace and they discussed whether the bridal party from Tewar could be fitted in. They went swiftly through bedrooms and halls, assessing the accommodation, and then emerged as the twilight was dissolving in splashes of purple and orange.

'Yes, this place should serve quite well as a guest-house,' Lindsay said with satisfaction as he put away his notes. 'Would you like to see the temple, while the servants get us some refreshments?'

The temple was dim inside, though hundreds of oil lamps burnt around the image of the goddess which was resplendent in priceless jewels and draped in a gold-embroidered sari. The chief priest came hurrying to greet them. Normally no person other than a Hindu was allowed inside, but here even the orthodox Brahmins regarded Sir Julian Lindsay as a native. When he walked barefoot into the white and green marble arcade, Caroline too removed her shoes and draped the veil of her hat more securely round her head like an *anchal*.

'Do you wish us to perform *puja*?' asked the chief priest, in Hindi.

'Not today. We shall come another time to worship, but today please say a prayer that the Crown Prince's wedding will be successful,' Lindsay replied, also in Hindi.

'That shall be done. It is the prayer of every Vijaypuri as well.'

At that moment the temple bells rang out for the evening ceremony of *arati*, when Jayder, a young priest, carried a silver tray laden with oil lamps and incense, coconut and flowers round the deity's image to invoke her blessings. Caroline stood silently beside Lindsay, watching the lovely ritual, and followed his example of touching the flame of the lamps and pressing the flame-warmed fingers to her eyes. He placed two silver coins for them on the tray, and bowed before they went out. They walked in silence but drawn together now by a magnetism stronger than words.

The royal retainers at Mahadev Vilas were waiting on the long terrace with trays of cool sherbet and sweets. The Resident informed them that the bridal party from Tewar would be housed there. 'Palace officials will be coming later to work out the details,' he explained, 'but I have to ascertain that the bridal party will be looked after. Any misunderstanding between the Maharaja of Tewar and the Crown Prince of Vijaypur would, have the widest repercussions. That is why I am taking a personal interest in the proceedings.'

The retainers left them alone as they sipped their sherbet and looked down to see the Vijaypur palace rise out of the lilac darkness like a fabulous jewel, every tower and turret a pinpoint of light, every veranda illuminated and the windows gleaming with the reflections. Further away, the town too twinkled as the townfolk lit their homes and shops. Darkness set in, and a gentle breeze blew round them.

Sitting on the terrace, Caroline felt she was floating on air. 'I don't feel like going down. It's so beautiful and ethereal here,' she said with a sigh, wishing she could sit there for ever with Julian Lindsay.

'Neither do I,' he replied gently. 'But we shall have to, before I lose my way on the hill paths.'

They rode down slowly, Lindsay stopping every now and then for Caroline, who was riding very carefully along the steep paths. After some time, they reached to the flat ground leading to the palace walls. Before passing through the gates, he came up closer to her and said, 'It has been a wonderful evening, Caroline. Thank you.' He said nothing more than a courteous 'Good evening' when they parted at the bridle-path.

In her room, Caroline looked at herself in the mirror and grimaced. Her riding-habit was crumpled and her hair dishevelled, but she was not really bothered because her eyes were sparkling and her new-found joy had brought a rosy warmth to her pale cheeks.

'Shall we have a double wedding next month?' Prince Kamal asked Lindsay when they met that evening at the Residency.

He frowned. 'Yes,' he said tersely. 'Your sister's and yours.'

'I wasn't referring to those,' the Prince said with a mischievous smile.

'Well, I was . . .' the Resident replied.

'Hmm. Well, perhaps you should not be seen saying evening prayers up there if you are not serious,' the Prince continued.

Lindsay looked at him, marvelling at the speed at which news was relayed. 'There is no frivolity in riding together or in showing the temple,' he countered defensively.

Prince Kamal shook his head and smiled again. Lindsay toyed with his pipe, remembering the enchantment of the violet hour on the hill. Seldom had he felt so attuned to the mood of another person. There had been no need to communicate through words because they could reach out to each other through deeper ways. He was surprised that he had been able to tell Caroline things that he had told no one else.

'How easily she understood what I left unsaid!' he marvelled, glancing at the part of the palace where she lived. 'What an unclouded instinct she has for perceiving things!'

Prince Kamal followed his gaze. 'Freedom can be dreary, Julian,' he said. 'It is time you relinquished it.'

The Resident smiled. 'Since you will be married shortly, it is just as well that you do not cherish your freedom!' He beckoned to one of the retainers to bring in champagne, with which they toasted their success with the Tewar party.

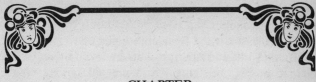

CHAPTER
ELEVEN

THE NEXT few weeks passed quickly while Caroline floated through days of a quiet joy. The evening on Devgiri Hill had transformed her. There was a radiance in her which was entirely new. People noticed and commented, but no one guessed the cause.

Everyone was soon involved in the preparations for the double wedding of Prince Kamal and Princess Padmini. The townsfolk took pride in decorating the main streets with arches covered by mango leaves and hanging festoons along the roads. A huge marquee was constructed on the main lawn where the wedding would take place, and chairs and sofas were brought from storerooms and placed inside it, with the guests' names embossed on the seats. Workers began constructing an earthen stove for the ceremonial fire required in every Hindu wedding. Masses of flowers were ordered from cities less arid than Vijaypur, and expert cooks from Lucknow, Delhi, Calcutta and Bombay arrived with their assistants. Crates of wine and champagne came from Calcutta, while trusted palace officials were sent to Lucknow, Bombay and Calcutta to purchase silks, satins, linen and saris. Jewellers from these cities came to sell their wares.

The Maharani enlisted her daughter and Caroline to help her to select gifts for the two brides. Caroline had never before seen such a collection of jewellery and sat there wondering if she were in Aladdin's cave. There were tiaras encrusted with nine types of gems; necklaces, bracelets and ear-rings clustered with rubies, diamonds and emeralds; rings with stones as large as robins' eggs designed with exquisite craftsmanship. Sitadevi's room glowed with the reflected light of the sparkling jewels.

The Maharani selected several beautiful pieces for Caroline, so that she could go properly adorned to the wedding. She was overwhelmed by the gifts and tried on the pieces with the excitement of a child. The Maharaja's concubines, except Pran Singh's mother, strolled in and made their purchases. The room twinkled as the gems caught the prisms of light.

It was evening when this pleasant work was over, and Caroline wandered out for a walk on the lawn. After some time she came to the gate which opened out to the graceful white house occupied by the Resident. She had an overwhelming urge to go there and see him, but knew that it would be highly improper, and an action he would be likely to criticise. So she stopped near the gardens of the Residency, thinking of its occupant. Pausing, she saw Lindsay and Richard Brooke emerge from the office looking tense and tired. Although Lindsay spoke kindly to Richard, the words, if they were of comfort, failed to dispel the tutor's gloom, because Richard kept shaking his head slowly as though refuting everything the other man said. After this short and inconclusive exchange, they shook hands and Richard walked slowly down the steps of the circular veranda, immersed in thought.

Caroline moved away, disturbed by what she had seen. In Calcutta, she had believed Richard to be excited by his new post in the Viceroy's office. Why did he seem to be so unhappy now, she wondered. Walking back to the palace, she recalled that throughout the week following their return from Calcutta, Richard had been strangely withdrawn, busy with his pupils and his own correspondence, which had suddenly swelled. He had already given his notice to the Resident and the Maharaja's Secretary.

Lindsay had appeared to receive the news with mixed feelings. He expressed regret that the Princes would be losing such an able tutor, but he was also glad that Richard had finally settled on a career which had changed him from a diffident man into a self-assured and confident one. Not once did he express his relief that Richard's departure would put an end to the romance between the tutor and Princess Padmini.

Thinking about her colleague and the Princess, Caroline strolled in the garden, admiring the lighting and decorations, until she came upon a secluded part of the grounds where she sat to rest her feet for a while. A rustle of silk roused her from her reveries, and, before she could move away, she saw the Princess and Richard sitting not far away under a flowering Flame of the Forest, its spreading branches and large scarlet flowers. But the inert evening air carried their voices clearly.

'So,' Padmini said in a husky voice, 'You have come to say goodbye.'

'Yes, my dear. I must go away before your wedding. I couldn't bear to see you marry someone else.' Richard spoke in the calm tone of a person who is resigned to unhappiness.

'You needn't see me marry Prince Uday!' she protested, her flashing dark eyes visible to Caroline. 'You could have agreed to my plan.'

'To run away together?' he asked gently, shaking his

head. 'That would not be the right way to start a new life. How far would we run? The disapproval of both your people and mine would always catch up with us?'

Padmini tossed her head. 'What do I care for them? I am a princess descended from the Sun God. I pay little heed to the idle chatter of the people,' she said imperiously.

'I know, my dear. That's why it's better like this,' Richard said gravely.

'Why is it better like this?' she asked suspiciously.

'Because we are separated not only by different countries, but by different ideas. Sir Julian was right, you know.'

'So you listened to Sir Julian! He always gets what he wants. We are all pawns on his political chess-board.' Padmini said with resentment.

Richard sighed. 'My dear, it's not that. We could never oppose everyone and still be happy.' He turned, and took her jewelled hands. 'I shall cherish my memories of you, Padmini.'

'But you will not share my life . . .' Padmini mused. 'Memories fade . . . but life goes on. And as you become involved in your life in Calcutta, in time even the memories will fade.'

'When you start your new life in Tewar, will you really think of me?' he asked harshly.

A silence fell between the young lovers while the wind sighed among the scarlet blossoms of the overhanging branches. Then Padmini began to cry softly, and Richard drew her close to him.

Caroline stole away, unwilling to hear more, for fear that her anger against the Resident would overwhelm her. 'So he arranged it thus!' she thought stormily, making her way back to her room. 'That is why he insisted that Richard should accompany me to Calcutta! And no doubt he asked the Viceroy to offer Richard a position at Government House, to take him away from Vijaypur before Padmini's marriage. How devious and determined!'

In her room, Caroline sat at the window, watching preparations for the two weddings with unseeing eyes as she remembered the dark head of the Princess against Richard's fair head, two hapless victims of the Resident's schemes. *Can he be so heartless?* Caroline wondered. *Could he deliberately separate two people who love each other?* Her resentment rose against him, and with this resentment was the painful knowledge that love meant little to him. He had no heart, only a cool and calculating head!

Richard left for Calcutta the next day. He took leave of Caroline in the little drawing-room downstairs where they used to take tea together after their classes. She was sad to see him go. Not only had he been a pleasant companion and colleague, he was also, in her opinion, a wronged man. How much she regretted her part in the Resident's game to separate the Princess and the tutor! Now as the slender young man stood before her, Caroline wanted to tell him to stay, even if it meant defying him.

As if divining her thoughts, Richard said wearily, 'Don't feel sorry for me, Caroline. It is better this way. We were both a little foolish and unrealistic for a while. Just as well we realised it in time—before taking some irrevocable step.'

'You can say it so calmly? Does it mean so little to you?' she cried indignantly.

He smiled. 'Dear, romantic Caroline! How naïve you

are! But that won't do, you know. You will have to grow up and accept things.' He paused, and spoke seriously. 'You too will have to set aside daydreaming and choose a realistic alternative.'

'I don't know what you mean, Richard,' she muttered, a vague disquiet clouding her mood.

'Yes, you do. Don't give your heart to Julian—that's what I mean. He lives in a different world. I doubt if there is room enough for you or any woman. Believe me, I know. I have known him for many years. If and when . . . a chance of happiness comes, grasp it, Caroline, before it's too late.'

Caroline understood what he referred to. 'Is that your philosophy—to drift from one attachment to another?' she asked coldly.

'Yes, if that is the way to avoid unhappiness,' Richard admitted.

'Nonsense! I do not accept such an attitude!' Caroline scoffed.

'Come, let us not argue . . . I have to be off in an hour. Well, my dear, look after yourself and be happy.' Richard said, shaking her hand and patting her cheek in a brotherly manner.

'Goodbye, Richard. When I go to Calcutta again, I shall look forward to seeing you.'

Richard nodded cheerfully and left the room with a brisk step. Caroline sat quietly for a while, pondering his advice.

That afternoon the first batches of guests began to arrive from various parts of Rajputana. She saw the colourful banners of Ajmer and Ramgarh, Chitor and Jodhpur, Udaipur and Bundi, as the cavalry and carriages of these princely states entered through the iron gates and clattered into the central courtyard. An entire wing of the Vijaypur palace had been set apart for them, while tents were pitched in far corners of the palace grounds to accommodate the officials and attendants accompanying the princely families. Every colour was represented in the fine lawn shirts and the gauzy turbans sported by the men. The voluminous mirror skirts and saris of the women twinkled and shimmered as they moved around the palace and gardens.

The princesses were too excited to study. When Caroline asked them to return to the classroom, they protested with one voice. 'No, Miss Caroline! Not until the wedding is over!'

She smiled indulgently. 'Very well, but remember, I expect you to perform your parts well before the guests tomorrow night. So don't forget to rehearse properly before you go on stage!'

As one, the girls agreed. For several weeks Caroline had worked with them to perfect their English recitations and songs, while the Indian music-teacher had made them rehearse the colourful ballads commemorating the beauty of Queen of Padmini of Chitor, the piety of Queen Meerabai of Mewar and the romance of Queen Samyukta of Delhi, along with the legends of valour and chivalry.

'Our brothers are missing Mr Brooke,' one of the princesses said with a sly smile. 'Why could he not have stayed on, at least till the wedding?'

'Because,' Caroline said as airily as she could, 'the Viceroy needed him soon.'

The girls giggled, not quite convinced. 'Tomorrow,' one of them announced, 'the Prince from Tewar, our half-sister's bridegroom, will arrive.'

'How nice,' Caroline replied briskly, as though she

saw no connection between Richard's departure and Prince Uday's arrival.

Next day, the bridal party from Tewar arrived. Caroline, surrounded by the princesses, watched them from the roof of the palace. The two eldest simpered and smiled, aware that their own marriages would happen quite soon, since their eldest half-sister was getting married at last. It had been a cause of relief to them that their seventeen-year-old half-sister was to leave home, otherwise they could not hope for the same.

'Which is Prince Uday of Tewar?' Caroline asked fourteen-year-old Princess Radha as the colourful procession reached the palace gates. Twenty horsemen clattered into the main square, their banners fluttering in the breeze, like the loose ends of their green and orange turbans.

'He will be in one of the carriages, Miss Caroline,' she replied. 'He is the bridegroom. We may not see him until the wedding. The bride of our brother is also in a carriage. I wonder what she looks like?'

Caroline saw that two gilt carriages were following behind, flying the green and orange colours of Tewar. The windows of the carriages were hung with strings of jasmine, that served as a floral screen to conceal the faces of the prince and princess from Tewar.

A short ceremony of welcome was performed in the grounds, with the lighting of lamps and blowing of conch-shells. Royal priests wafted incense and scattered flower petals around the two carriages before they rolled away again out of the palace gates and towards the Devgiri Hill. Twenty tall horsemen preceded the carriages, while the curricles and landaus followed.

Late in the afternoon, Caroline saw the flags of Tewar flying over the minarets of Mahadev Vilas where she and

Lindsay had sipped sherbet on an evening that had held magic for her.

How far away that man seemed, thought Caroline as her eyes rested on the hilltop palace. For there was the husband he had chosen for Padmini, a man she had never seen and could not possibly like. To the Resident, that was irrelevant. And what of the Princess Indumati, the sixteen-year-old girl who was to marry Kamal of Vijaypur? Was she, like Padmini, awaiting with dread the wedding with a man she had never seen? No, Caroline thought, Indumati would be looking forward to her marriage with a handsome, kindly prince because she had not given her heart to someone else.

Thoughts of Padmini's predicament darkened Caroline's mood as she dressed for the banquet that the Maharaja of Vijaypur was holding in honour of the Maharaja of Tewar and the other guests.

The vast reception hall had been done up for the occasion. Furniture gleamed with new polish, and the upholsteries of satin and brocade seemed to have acquired a new sheen. Flowers had been placed in countless Spode and Dresden china vases and bowls. Five splendid chandeliers glistened as they caught the light of the candles. The polished marble floors gleamed like glass where the heavy Persian carpets did not cover them.

Caroline hesitantly entered the reception hall, feeling a little lost amid the glittering gathering of Indian nobility. Seeing the familiar face of Mrs Dalrymple at one end of the room, She walked towards her and curtsied. The wife of the commanding officer acknowledged her presence with the merest nod, coldly appraising Caroline's elegant dress of dull gold brocade made from material presented to her by the Maharani. A simple gold chain with a topaz locket—also given by Sitadevi—encircled her throat. Her rich auburn hair stood out in contrast to the muted richness of her dress.

At once Caroline regretted having approached Matilda Dalrymple. Lydia stood next to her mother, wearing a pink dress of frothy organdie, aloof from and indifferent to her surroundings.

In an attempt at polite conversation, Caroline said, 'I have never beheld such splendour as we see among the Indian nobility.'

Mrs Dalrymple lifted an eyebrow. 'Do you really think so, Miss Emerson? I find it rather overwhelming.'

Lydia chimed in. 'Most definitely. Such an unrestrained display of wealth!'

Caroline looked away, wondering how she could leave the two ladies without discourtesy, when she saw the Resident walk across towards them. He looked very distinguished in his elegant white evening dress with a red sash across his broad chest and several decorations on his lapel. When his dark blue eyes shone appreciatively at her, she could not help the gladness surging within her.

When he was at their side, Lindsay bowed courteously to Mrs Dalrymple and the two younger women.

'Well, Miss Dalrymple,' he asked the beaming Lydia. 'How do you like the princely party?'

Aware of the Resident's appreciation for Indian customs, Lydia praised the colour and richness of the gathering with a fulsomeness that astonished Caroline, who had noted the young lady's earlier derisive observations.

'And you, Caroline?' he asked, his face softening. 'How have you been? I have not seen you since our . . . expedition to Devgiri Hill.'

She felt her cheeks glowing with pleasure and gladness. 'So he too remembered that magical evening,' she
thought. 'And he called me by my Christian name!' 'I
. . . have been busy . . . with my pupils,' she murmured
as his ardent gaze rested on her lips and eyes, and swept
over her gracefully curved figure. 'They will perform
tomorrow before the guests.'

'They will, I hope, do you proud,' he said in a low
voice.

'I am sure they will,' Caroline said quietly.

The words between them seemed irrelevant because
their eyes were eloquent with other messages. Mrs
Dalrymple glanced from one to the other, frowning.
Intercepting that glance, Caroline blushed, fully aware
of the older woman's reactions.

'Please excuse me, Mrs Dalrymple, Sir Julian,' she
said hurriedly. 'I remember something I have to do.' She
made a move to go, but the Resident detained her by
holding her arm.

'A moment, Caroline. I have something to tell you
. . . A message from the Maharani.' He bowed to the
two other women and led her out of the dazzling hall to a
secluded terrace near by, where lamps glowed on flowering camellia and jasmine bushes.

Mrs Dalrymple and Lydia watched them leave the
room together with surprise and dismay. When Matilda
looked at her daughter, she saw that her temper was
rising.

Gaining the terrace, Lindsay drew up a chair for
Caroline. 'I was wondering if you had run away,' he said
in a tender voice. 'I have not seen you for a week.'

Caroline felt her heart beating wildly as he gazed
steadily at her. The noise of the reception receded, and
the heady scent of camellias was all around them. He

reached out to pluck a cluster of the white flowers, and put them in her hand. She trembled at his touch.

'Camellias for Caroline,' he murmured. 'How often have I looked at the flowers in my garden and thought of you. But, tell me, where have you been? I have not had even a glimpse of you since that evening.'

'I . . . saw . . . you,' she said in an unsteady voice. 'You were talking to Richard on your veranda.'

'Did you? Why did you not join us?'

'Richard seemed unhappy . . . I did not want to intrude. He left the next day.'

'He will not be unhappy for long,' Lindsay said quietly. 'He will find new interests and be . . . grateful that I sent him away.'

All the joy in Caroline's heart vanished with those words. *Can he really be so cold and calculating? Does he manipulate everyone? Will he send me away too if I become a problem?* she wondered with rising panic.

'What is it, Caroline?' he asked, perplexed by the sudden change in her countenance.

'You do not deny that you sent Richard away—deliberately?'

The Resident frowned. 'Of course not. Why should I? It was the wisest thing to do, under the circumstances.'

'Wisest for whom, Sir Julian?' Caroline asked coldly.

His face became grave. 'For Richard, for Padmini, and those whose lives are linked to them,' he replied evenly.

'Have you any idea how much heartache your wisdom has caused to those two?'

Lindsay inclined his head to one side with an ironic smile. 'Have I?'

'Do you not know? Or do you not care? Is it in the end only the fate of Vijaypur which matters? And, of course, your rôle in it! Those who come between you and your plans must be swept aside. Do you realise, Sir Julian, that in your own way you are as whimsical and arbitrary as the Maharaja?'

Caroline spoke hurriedly and with evident distress, but even then she noticed that his lips tightened and the fire went out of his eyes.

'Your compassion does you credit, Caroline,' he said quietly. 'I had not realised you held such high opinions about me. Thank you for being so candid. For a . . . time . . . I thought I had met a woman who had some understanding.' Though his voice was cool, the tenderness that had shone in his face as he had greeted her remained. 'But, before I take you back to the reception, you might like to see something. Come,' he commanded gently, striding ahead of her. Caroline followed until they came to a moonlit veranda.

Lindsay stopped abruptly and held out a finger towards a stone bench shrouded in darkness. 'There is your heartbroken princess. Have a good look at her and tell me if she is ready to commit *johar!*'

Caroline saw Padmini sitting demurely next to a distinguished, aquiline-featured man, gazing up at him as he spoke. There was no passion between them, but there was an excitement in her eyes and a gentleness in his as they conversed hesitantly.

'I forced the Maharani to agree to this meeting between the bride and bridegroom—before the wedding— which is quite against orthodox Hindu tradition. But I did it—risking displeasure in some circles so that our Princess could have the freedom to reject the match if she so chose.'

Caroline watched them, wondering whether she should laugh or cry. She turned to the Resident and said uncertainly, 'Perhaps she has accepted the inevitable gracefully . . . After all, Richard has gone.'

'Yes, and quite happily too, I gather. From what I hear, he was excited by the offer to work in Calcutta. Had he had any real regrets, he would not have left so swiftly.'

Caroline bowed her head. 'Have I misunderstood everything?' she asked in a low voice.

'I think you have, Caroline. I wonder if you really know the difference between love and infatuation?'

She raised sparkling emerald eyes to his mocking sapphire ones. 'Of course I do!' she protested.

'I hope you do,' Julian murmured a moment before his arms went round her slender waist, drawing her close to him. He raised one hand, caressing her hair and neck, and then traced her eyes, nose and lips with a long cool fingers, smiling with just a hint of amusement at her bewildered expression.

Caroline struggled ineffectually to release herself from that embrace, when Sir Julian's lips captured hers in a long burning kiss. She felt a flame leaping within her, rising to meet the fire she felt in his lips and arms. For one moment she stiffened and then reluctantly but joyfully melted into the embrace. His kiss became wild and possessive and then tender once more. His hands moved over her bare shoulders and neck, slid down her cool arms, and then back to her burning cheeks. He could feel her heart beat against his, her breasts rising and falling under the brocade bodice.

Then, as he felt the tang of salty tears on his lips, he released her and she moved away at once, trembling and leaning on the balustrade for support. He scanned her face, perplexed to find her eyes brimming over with tears.

'Caroline,' he murmured, 'have I offended you?'

She shook her head, without looking at him. 'Are you trying to tell me something, Sir Julian?' she whispered hoarsely. 'I am afraid I am not accustomed to these amorous antics.'

'Caroline,' he said gently. 'These are not antics. Can you not recognise . . .'

'Resident Saheb!' the Maharaja's second son called out in his smooth voice.

Lindsay turned round, frowning at the young Prince whose smile was far from apologetic. 'Yes, Prince, what is it?'

Pran Singh bowed elaborately. 'My father wants you to be present in the reception hall. The boring speeches are about to begin.'

'I shall join you presently,' the Resident replied, without a trace of embarrassment at being found in a difficult situation with a young lady.

Pran Singh smiled contemptuously and moved back into the shadows from which he had emerged.

'Will you come with me?' Sir Julian asked Caroline, who was standing with her face averted towards the shadowy garden.

'No,' she said unsteadily, impatiently brushing away tears of vexation. 'I would rather not.'

'My dear,' he said in a voice which seemed to caress her, even though she bristled with indignation. 'I never meant to . . . let it happen . . . this way.'

'That is astonishing,' replied Caroline, steeling herself against the spell of his voice and touch. 'I thought you did nothing without deliberate intention.'

Sir Julian laughed, and, taking her hand, kissed it, his eyes on hers, mocking and challenging. 'Sometimes the wisest of us do foolish things. If you give me a little of your time tomorrow, I shall explain.'

He did not wait for an answer, but with firm and unhurried steps he walked back to the dazzling reception hall, once more the grave and authoritative Resident of Vijaypur.

Caroline stood on the dark terrace for some time, trying to calm her trembling limbs and disturbed spirits while wondering whether Sir Julian was at heart a capricious lothario who alternated between tenderness and derision. Yet the memory of his kiss and gentleness belied such as idea. Sighing deeply, she walked slowly towards her apartment to tidy herself before returning to the reception hall.

Walking along the length of the terrace, Caroline passed the tall french windows of the hall and saw him standing by the Crown Prince while a courtier read out a speech. She marvelled at Lindsay's perfect composure. She determined to return to the reception as calm and serene as he.

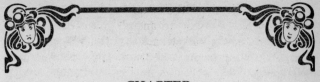

CHAPTER
TWELVE

A DUCK SHOOT had been organised for the following morning. It was still dark when the shooting party began to assemble on the opposite bank of Lake Rashmi. The sky was a graded canopy of rose, lilac and blue blending with a veil of mist rising from the lake. At that tranquil hour, the ducks sat motionless on the large sandy stretch, splashes of varied colours in the blue-grey dawn. They squatted in their hundreds, unaware of their impending doom. When the mist began to lift, the birds flapped their wings to greet what would be their last day.

Princess Padmini and Caroline went up to the roof of the palace to see the spectacle. A bright canopy had been erected on the opposite banks of the lake for the guests to rest and have refreshments. The Rajput chiefs had donned western clothes and instead of the colourful turbans all of them wore the white sola topi with a wide brim at the back. Using her binoculars, Caroline spotted Lindsay riding towards the other bank astride a powerful chestnut horse. He and Prince Kamal rode on either side of the Maharaja of Tewar. They made a magnificent trio: Caroline felt her heart swelling with pride. Reluctantly she passed the binoculars to Padmini, who was waiting impatiently to train the glasses further down on the solitary figure of Prince Uday riding behind his brother with an easy grace. Padmini smiled and sighed, convincing her governess that she had taken to her betrothed.

The two young women watched the shooting party assemble on the broad sandy banks and organise themselves. The ducks were now floating or paddling among the reeds which filled the other side of the lake.

'Oh those pretty, pretty birds,' Padmini cried. 'Why must they all be shot? They have done no harm. My mother was against this and suggested that a tiger hunt be organised instead, but Sir Julian said he did not want the guests to be taken too far from here.'

'Why?' Caroline asked, disturbed.

'Who knows?' the Princess replied, shrugging her shoulders. Then she, too, felt uneasy and turned to Caroline with a frown. 'Do you think the Resident is being unduly anxious about the weddings?'

'Of course he is,' Caroline replied soothingly. 'Your marriages will form a strong alliance with the powerful state of Tewar. He does not want anything untoward to happen.'

Padmini smiled. 'Poor Sir Julian! How much he is missing of life! Instead of enjoying his position and taking his pleasure, he worries about other people's marriages, the repercussions of alliances and the relationships of Indian princes with Whitehall!' She glanced speculatively at Caroline as she spoke.

'Perhaps his work gives him great pleasure—People want different things from life.'

The Princess nodded. 'I suppose you are right. Anyway he has helped me to see what I want of life.'

'Has he?' Caroline asked, surprised.

'Oh yes,' Padmini replied softly, looking at the figure of Uday Singh in the distance. 'Perhaps I have always wanted it, and because I felt it would never come my way

I resorted to unorthodox remedies. Sir Julian was astute enough to see this.'

Caroline stared at her pupil in some perplexity. 'And I argued with him from the first in your defence!'

'I know, dear Miss Caroline, and that is why we all love you. Instead of pleasing the most powerful man in Vijaypur, you chose to antagonise him!' She dimpled prettily, her eyes full of mischief. 'And of course he was drawn to you, because of that.'

'Was he?' Caroline murmured.

'You know he was . . . Sir Julian has not met a woman like you before . . . with such fire and sweetness at once. I wish I could be like you, or my mother. Our patience and gentleness is so abused. For years I have seen my mother unhappy and wondered if I, too, would meet the same fate. That is perhaps why I wanted to escape . . . with Richard. But today . . . I am glad I didn't. I am happy as things are, because . . .'

A cry of pain cut through Padmini's reveries. The Princess stood frozen by the balustrade, then slowly turned to see a cluster of several men near the sandbanks on the other side of Lake Rashmi.

'What was that?' Caroline asked, staring at the scene before her. Fighting a terrible fear, she whispered, 'Let us go down and see.'

Both of them ran down the stairs from the roof, along corridors and down more stairs until they were on the ground floor, gasping. The sight that greeted them almost took away their breath.

Lindsay and the Maharaja of Tewar were, between them, carrying an unconscious Prince Kamal towards the long veranda where the two girls stood, horrified. Seeing them, Lindsay barked out an order. 'Get a cot, immediately!'

Caroline turned to find a crowd of servants standing around them. She beckoned to four retainers to follow her to the small sitting-room near by where there was a light couch on which the Prince could be carried to his room. When Caroline returned with the servants carrying the couch, Padmini was already at her brother's side, wiping the blood off his face and hands with the end of her silk sari, while tears streamed down her pale cheeks. She stood aside as Lindsay and the Maharaja gently laid Prince Kamal down.

The Resident again commanded quietly, and then, glancing round, beckoned to Caroline. 'Follow the Prince and never leave him for a second. I am coming.'

She nodded grimly, and then followed the couch, with the Princess walking swiftly at her side.

Lindsay spoke calmly to the distraught Maharaja of Tewar. 'Please return to the shoot, Your Highness, and don't say or do anything until I have the doctor's advice.'

'Such a terrible thing, Sir Julian,' the elderly Maharaja said. 'Who could have done this evil thing?'

He breathed deeply. 'I will shortly tell you, sir. Please be patient till then,' he said and strode off the veranda to fetch Dr Williams, the Anglo-Indian physician attached to the Vijaypur Lancers.

When he returned ten minutes later, he found everyone talking in whispers around the wounded Prince. Only the Maharani was sitting and crying softly, holding her son's hands, though the Prince kept murmuring, 'Mother, I'm all right!'

Dr Williams came in, outwardly calm but obviously anxious, and made the necessary examination. Then, with a wan smile, he turned to the Resident and said, 'You were right, sir. It's a superficial cut, despite the profuse bleeding . . . which is already slowing down. No artery has been severed. Now if all of you will stand aside, I shall attend to the Prince's wounds.'

Everyone moved away to the chairs around the room, leaving the doctor free to do his work of cleaning the wound and dressing it, with the assistance of the Maharani.

Lindsay went to assure the bride's father that all was well, and to calm the guests and ask them to continue the programme arranged for them. He then informed the Maharaja of Vijaypur of the incident. What transpired at that encounter no one knew, though retainers reported that the Resident appeared grim and tight-lipped as he left the Maharaja's apartments. On his return to the Prince's room, he found him sitting, propped up on pillows, with a bandage round his shoulder. Sitadevi fanned him with a palmyra leaf, though a servant was busily pulling the punkah cords that worked the wooden fan overhead.

As he entered, the Maharani rose in great agitation. 'Sir Julian!' she said with a catch in her voice. 'How can I ever thank you for saving my son's life?'

The Resident smiled wanly, remembering the strange, swift instinct which made him pull Prince Kamal aside just as he heard a bullet whizzing through the air. It had missed the Prince's neck, but grazed his shoulder, causing bleeding and shock. The Prince looked at him gravely.

'It was not a shooter's stray bullet, was it, Julian?' he asked.

'No, Kamal,' he replied, shaking his head. 'It was not an innocent bullet aimed at the ducks. It was a deliberate attempt to stop the two weddings—by killing either you or me.'

The Maharani gasped. 'But suppose the man tries again?' she asked in a quivering voice.

Lindsay sighed. 'We shall be careful. I have already sent word to Colonel Dalrymple to alert the Lancers and post additional guards in the palace. Kamal and Padmini should stay in their apartments until the wedding—as custom demands,' he said with a wry smile.

'And you?' Caroline said clearly in the hushed room. 'What precautions will you take?' No sooner had she asked this than she regretted it, and a crimson stain appeared on her pale cheeks.

He directed a long and tender glance towards her. 'I shall be careful, Miss Emerson,' he said softly, touched by her spontaneous concern.

Caroline, however, turned away, busying herself by tidying strips of bandage and ice-packs scattered on a near-by table.

'Who is behind this?' Prince Kamal asked the Resident.

'Can't you guess? Your half-brother, Pran Singh.'

'I might have known! But would he dare show his hand?'

'His ambition knows no bounds,' Lindsay said grimly. 'But we must not let him frighten us into submitting to him. You, Prince Kamal, must fight for your rights.'

'Even if we are killed in the process?' Padmini asked.

Lindsay nodded. 'Yes, even then. The world, Princess, belongs to the brave. At least, so your scriptures say.' He looked slowly at everyone in turn. 'Please remember to be careful—until tomorrow?' Then, bowing, he left the room.

As Caroline saw the door close, anxiety overcame her. Excusing herself, she went out and stood in the sunlit corridor. Hearing footsteps, Sir Julian turned as she walked slowly towards him.

'Yes, Caroline?' he said gently.

'Was . . . the bullet meant for you?'

He gazed thoughtfully out of the marble-latticed windows. 'No, I think it was intended for Kamal, but I would have served equally well as a target. After all, if Kamal were dead, I should not be able to push through my plans for progress.'

'Then Pran Singh might aim at you next?'

'Possibly.'

Caroline shuddered. 'You will . . . be careful?'

Sir Julian's eyes moved slowly over her pale anxious face and red-rimmed eyes, and the simple yellow dress moulded to the gentle curves of her body. 'If you wish me to be careful,' he said huskily, moving closer.

She nodded, the anger and resentment of last night wiped out by the gentle expression on his face. There was no irony or banter in his tone.

'About last night . . . I'm sorry.'

'Are you?' Caroline asked softly, lowering her eyes, wishing he had not apologised for his kisses.

'I meant to tell you . . . many things . . .'

She looked up to see him regarding her with a sudden, urgent tenderness. 'What things?' she whispered.

'This evening . . . I shall tell you. Will you meet me in the Maharani's private sitting-room?' he asked with a joyous eagerness.

'I shall.'

Sir Julian took her hand and kissed it, and then slowly walked away. Caroline felt her heart dancing, despite the surrounding gloom. She returned to the Crown Prince's apartment to assist the Maharani.

An uneasy stillness fell over the palace, despite the

Resident's injunction to maintain every sign of normality. Everything, he commanded, was to continue according to schedule. Though forced at first, the pretence of normality did indeed restore some semblance of it. The guests, shocked at first by the accident, were glad to have the entertainment to take their minds off the unpleasant events. Perhaps some of them might even have contemplated returning to their homes but for his insistence that to do so would diminish the prestige of one of their ancient Rajput houses and invite the scorn and derision of others.

Boat-trips had been arranged on Lake Rashmi, with a sumptuous lunch arranged in the cool marble rooms of Lotus Mahal. The April heat did not touch the guests as they sat to eat at the small tables, while the water lapped round them. After a short rest, they assembled again in the late afternoon to watch a polo game organised by Colonel Dalrymple. Throwing caution to the winds, Princess Padmini and Caroline stood on a secluded terrace on the third floor to watch. Prince Kamal had protested irritably against his incarceration, but his mother had supported the Resident's advice that he should not go out.

The two young women, holding parasols over their heads, watched the game as the riders of the Vijaypur Lancers played against some of the equally skilled guests. Lindsay joined the Rajput side, while Dalrymple played with the Lancers. There were shouts of success and victory, of exasperation and annoyance as horses and riders thundered over the ground, now bending, now straightening up again to make it to the winning-post. As twilight fell, the game ended, and the guests were conducted to their apartments to bath and dress before the evening entertainment.

After the game, still in his riding clothes, the Resident looked in to see how Prince Kamal was faring, and was relieved to find him much recovered, although his mother said that he had slept only fitfully during the afternoon. Princess Padmini was surprised to see him looking weary and dispirited, when an hour earlier he had been so cheerful and energetic on the polo ground.

'I am glad our side won,' she said softly. 'Caroline and I were impressed by your skill.'

Lindsay did not reply, but after some time asked in a harsh tone that bewildered the Princess, 'Where is Caroline?'

'She is preparing a pudding for Kamal,' Sitadevi replied.

'Would you ask her to see me at my house, an hour later than we arranged?'

Both the Maharani and Padmini were surprised by this unconventional request from a man who was so intent upon propriety.

'Could you not meet her in my private sitting-room,' the Maharani asked, 'as you had planned earlier?'

'No, that will not be possible. Please ask her to come to the Residency—accompanied by a maid, of course.'

When he had left, Padmini smiled. 'You know, Mother, I do believe the formidable Resident has been humbled at last!'

Sitadevi sighed. 'I hope he will behave kindly. Such strong-willed men can be difficult.'

The Princess laughed softly, jubilant at the thought that the English dragon was beginning to be tamed. She conveyed the message with sighs and simpers until Caroline blushed and became clumsy with the dish of custard she had brought in for the Prince.

CHAPTER
THIRTEEN

LEAVING THEM to minister to the Prince, Caroline hurried to her room. She pulled half a dozen dresses from the closet until she found an ethereal one of green chiffon. She wore her mother's pearls, put a wreath of fresh camellias round her hair and practically waltzed down the stairs to the palace grounds which were now crowded with the wedding guests, her maid following more sedately.

'What will he say?' Caroline thought, with excitement tugging at her as they walked towards the Residency. 'How will he say it, I wonder?' The thought of being swept into his arms and kissed long and ardently made the colour rush to her cheeks. Thus with flushed cheeks and sparkling eyes, Caroline was ushered into the Resident's austere and elegant drawing-room, while her maid waited on the veranda.

He was already there, dressed impeccably in white coat-tails and black trousers, tight-lipped and cold-eyed. Caroline drew back in astonishment to see him look at her with such a bleak expression.

'No doubt you are aware of why I made the singular request for you to come here, Miss Emerson,' he said coldly.

Caroline could only shake her head in growing confusion and dismay. Lindsay's penetrating glance added to her bewilderment. Was this the man who had spoken so tenderly that morning?

'This afternoon, while I was playing polo, a visitor arrived from Calcutta,' he said, pausing to see the affect his announcement would have. 'A visitor who has come to see you only.'

'Who is it, Sir Julian?' Caroline asked softly.

The Resident retreated to the table where a drinks tray had been set. He helped himself generously to a glass of whisky. Then, turning to her, he said, 'The Honourable Edward Lockwood.'

Caroline shook her head. 'You can't be serious!'

His expression was inscrutable, as he said quietly, 'I am entirely serious. Edward Lockwood has come to see you.'

'Edward Lockwood?' Caroline repeated, astonished.

Lindsay nodded silently, his gaze more piercing than ever. Under the relentless scrutiny of his eyes, Caroline blushed, and hated herself for doing so, because he would misunderstand the cause of the sudden rush of colour to her cheeks. He placed the glass of whisky on a table, and came close to her.

'Miss Emerson,' he said in a weary voice, 'I must beg your pardon for . . . troubling you with my . . . occasional attentions. Had you but indicated that you had a suitor and were practically engaged to be married, I would have . . . behaved differently. As I was in complete ignorance of the situation, I can only ask to be excused for . . . whatever has happened.'

Caroline was speechless; once more he misunderstood her silence.

For a moment he stared at her, thinking how lovely she looked in the green chiffon dress which she had no doubt worn to please the Honourable Edward

Lockwood. The idea stirred up a sudden anger in him.

'No doubt I am at fault, Miss Emerson,' he continued gruffly. 'But it was the price you paid for not being frank about your forthcoming marriage. Why you did not disclose the fact is a great mystery to me. Was it to . . . encourage me to . . . make a fool of myself?'

Caroline was recovering from her bewilderment to find herself in a powerful rage. She was just going to tell him that she was not engaged to the Honourable Edward Lockwood when that gentleman walked into the drawing-room.

'Caro! My dear!' Edward exclaimed, moving towards her to clasp both her hand in his. He looked into her eyes and slowly kissed her hands. 'Are you surprised, Caro?' he murmured.

Her bewildered gaze moved from the fair head bowed before her to the dark one, near the window, towering over them both. She was perplexed by the blazing fury in Lindsay's eyes, which soon turned to desolation. Her gaze remained fixed on those deep blue eyes even while the grey eyes looked at her expectantly.

'I shall leave you together,' Lindsay said formally, striding out of his drawing-room.

'Well, Caro? Did I surprise you?'

'Yes, Edward,' she replied dully.

The young man laughed. 'Would you believe it, Caro? I was about to embark for England, when the Viceroy received a telegram to say that my uncle had passed away.'

'I am sorry to hear about your uncle,' Caroline said politely. 'But why have you come here?' she added, more coldly.

Edward smiled at her. 'You know why, Caro.'

'No, I don't know!' she cried, exasperated.

Edward continued to look very pleased. 'I want to return to England, with you as my wife.'

For the second time in the evening Caroline was lost for words. 'You can't mean that, Edward!' she whispered, amazed.

He nodded indulgently. 'I had intended to tell you . . . of my sentiments, in Calcutta, but somehow the con-founded Merton girls were always in the way.'

'You allowed the Merton girls to come in the way of such a momentous declaration?' Caroline asked angrily.

'Oh, Caro, it was not like that! I was planning to visit Vijaypur . . . but Uncle's death expedited my decision. You see,' he said triumphantly, 'Uncle Herbert left me a very handsome fortune.'

'You are now your own master; is that it?' she asked scornfully.

'Something like that,' he agreed, missing the angry glint in her eyes. 'Shall we discuss our plans?' He paused to smile. 'It is rather symbolic, don't you think, that I should arrive in the midst of a wedding?'

Before Caroline could reply, she heard the Resident's footsteps on the veranda outside the drawing-room. She turned to see him enter. 'Lockwood,' he said coldly, 'I think it is time for us to go to the reception at the palace. As my guest, you are required to attend.'

'Certainly, Sir Julian. I suppose Caro can come with us?'

'No!' Caroline said hastily. 'I must stay with the princesses, who are performing tonight.'

'I think,' Lindsay said icily, 'they will manage quite well without you, Miss Emerson. Why not stay with Mr Lockwood?'

'No,' Caroline replied stubbornly. 'I must be with the princesses.'

Without another word, she swiftly left the room and called to her maid. She was half running out of the Residency grounds until she had to negotiate the narrow opening in the bougainvillaeas which led to the palace gardens. When the climbers caught at her floating skirts, she tugged impatiently and moved on, as if the hounds of hell were pursuing her.

Champagne was being served in the gorgeous Durbar Hall. The two bridegrooms—Prince Kamal and Prince Uday—were dressed in Rajput costume, while the male guests wore western evening dress. Caroline sought shelter behind the Maharani, who sat on a sofa, watching. Around her were other ladies, heavily veiled and jewelled. The two brides—Padmini and Indumati—were in an upstairs room listening to music and submitting to the traditional teasing of a wedding eve. There was a murmur as the tall and imperious Resident Saheb entered the hall, followed by the fair and smiling Edward Lockwood.

As they took their seats, the young princes and princesses trooped in to sing songs and recite poems and ballads. The Rajput chiefs looked on, amused.

When the children had left, Edward sought Caroline out from the cluster of Rajput ladies, who giggled among themselves at the frank interest the English saheb was showing in the governess.

'Do be circumspect, Edward!' Caroline murmured. 'The Rajputs are very orthodox—unlike the Bengalis.'

He laughed. 'Really, Caroline, we are not in London, you know. I thought all those ideas of stiff social behaviour could be discarded here.'

'No, they cannot be!' she retorted, freeing her hand from his.

'Shall we go to the terrace and talk? I have little to say to the dear Maharaja.'

'No, I must stay here.'

Edward looked at her, puzzled. 'You might show more enthusiasm about my arrival, Caro,' he said patiently. 'To hear you, one would think you were annoyed by my presence!'

There was such frank injury in the young man's voice that Caroline was moved to say, 'It's not that, Edward. We've had a hard day, and I am tired. Why don't you try to talk to the guests, while I attend the Maharani?'

'Attend the Maharani?' he asked warmly. 'Don't talk as if you were a servant here, Caro! I won't have the future Countess of Elverston referred to in that way!'

'Future Countess of Elverston? What on earth are you talking about?'

Edward smiled. 'My elder brother is now the Earl, but he has so far produced six daughters. If he should die . . . without an heir, I shall succeed to the Earldom of Elverston. And you will be the Countess,' he added in a slow, meaningful manner.

Caroline's eyes emitted green fire. 'You are very sure of yourself, aren't you, Edward?' she asked icily. 'As it so happens, I *am* an employee of the Maharaja, and am quite happy to be one.'

Exasperated, Edward closed his eyes. 'Caro,' he said wearily, 'why make all this fuss when we both know what we are destined for?'

Before Caroline could make an appropriate riposte, Lindsay joined them. 'I hope I am not intruding,' he said in a toneless voice. 'But I do feel, Lockwood, that you should join me in conversation with the Rajput princes. They might take it amiss if you do not.'

Edward reluctantly left Caroline, in order to be introduced to the Rajput chiefs. She sighed, and asked herself, 'How am I to deal with this new situation?'

The evening's dilemma was solved by the announcement that Gulab-Bibi, the famed courtesan from Lucknow, and her troupe were going to dance for the gentlemen. Edward showed no reluctance to join Lindsay in attending the *mushaira*, or music session. Caroline fancied that the Resident smiled sarcastically at his enthusiasm, and she seethed inwardly. Yet she was grateful enough to escape from the Durbar Hall and repair to the zenana, where Padmini and Indubai were listening to plaintive songs of Sita and Savitri, the two ideals of Hindu womanhood.

The older ladies had now joined them. The singer raised her voice to drown the jingling of anklets, the hectic sounds of the table and the clanging harmonium accompanying Gulab-Bibi's dancing. The Rajput noblewomen pretended to be deaf to the laughter and appreciative cries of their menfolk emanating from the entertainment room. Inwardly they wondered what small fortunes were being expended by their menfolk to please one of Gulab-Bibi's novices.

In her amusement, Caroline forgot her own dilemma. She watched the sheen of saris and the glitter of jewels on the pale-coloured ladies until the April warmth made her doze off in the crowded room.

She awoke to find herself alone. For a moment she was confused, and then, hearing the sound of fireworks, she went out onto the balcony and saw that the dark summer sky was illuminated by a shower of stars. The Rajput ladies stood watching the display with the eager delight of children.

Anxious to escape the stifling closeness of the crowded balcony, Caroline went down into the garden.

There she saw Lindsay standing by himself, indifferent to the firework display as he smoked a pipe, looking absently towards the mid-distance.

'I shall go to him now,' she thought with rising excitement, 'and explain everything. I shall tell him that I have no intention of marrying Edward, or ever had any desire to do so after arriving in Vijaypur. I will tell him that I love . . . only him!'

Gathering courage, her heart pounding, Caroline walked slowly towards the Resident of Vijaypur.

'Sir Julian!' Caroline called out urgently. He turned, a question in his eyes.

'Yes, Miss Emerson?' he said, surprised.

'I . . . want . . . to tell . . . you that . . .' her eager and hurried words faded into silence as Miss Lydia Dalrymple glided towards the Resident in a pink gossamer gown, favouring Caroline with a curt nod.

'Sir Julian,' Lydia murmured, 'Papa says he wants to stay on, but mama and I are quite fatigued. Would you escort us home? We would feel so much safer with you.'

Lindsay nodded, but continued to gaze at Caroline with an inscrutable expression for some more moments. Then he asked in a gentle voice, almost an entreaty, 'What was it you wished to tell me?'

In a rush of joyous relief, Caroline was about to ask him to hear her in private for a minute when Lydia said in a voice thickened by jealousy,

'Am I intruding, Sir Julian? It seems the Teacher miss saheb has a message of great import for you. A very odd hour for imparting news, but no doubt she has adopted the habits of the palace.'

Caroline's eyes blazed. All the pent-up resentment of the past months overflowed, as she said, 'Insolent girl! How dare you talk to me in this fashion? Can you not learn to control your ill-bred impulses, at least while speaking to me?'

Lydia was astonished at first, but she knew that in order to prevent a *tête-à-tête* between the Resident and the governess she must infuriate the latter still more. With this in view, she laughed a laugh of mirthless contempt. 'How quickly you have acquired the airs of a lady, Miss Caroline! Is it in anticipation of future hopes?'

Out of all patience, Caroline fled from the lawn before her anger forced her to talk in a manner beneath her dignity. Had she but heard Lindsay call out her name in evident agitation, she would have turned back at once and accomplished her original intention, but his cry was drowned by the crackle of the fireworks. When she turned to climb the stairs, she saw him walking towards the palace gates with Lydia Dalrymple's arm in his.

Tears pricking her eyes, Caroline ran until she gained her room, where she flung herself on her bed to surrender to a tempest of anger and disappointment keener than anything she had experienced before.

'He was going to tell me something momentous tonight,' she sobbed. 'But everything has gone wrong! Oh, dear God, how can I escape from this predicament?' Still worrying, she fell at last into a troubled sleep.

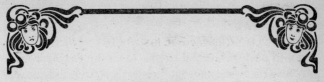

CHAPTER
FOURTEEN

Dawn danced into Vijaypur to the strains of shehnais
playing the *Bhari-Ravi* raga, awaking everyone to the
wedding day of Prince Kamal and Princess Padmini. The
music had begun before dawn when the morning star
glittered against a purple sky.

At first the music of the shehnai blended into
Caroline's dreams. Then she woke, and rising swiftly
went to her window to see the dawn break. Lake
Rashmi was clear and still as a mirror, reflecting Lotus
Mahal in all its iridescent glory. As the sky lightened
from purple to lilac to rose, the tempo of the shehnai also
quickened, flounced and frolicked as if keeping rhythm
with some invisible dancer's feet. The gaiety however
was superficial. Beneath it lay a bittersweet quality, of
partings and farewells. It echoed the mood of the two
brides who were leaving their homes to begin a new
life.

Caroline leaned out of the window as the mournful
strains of the shehnai plucked at her heart and stirred up
longings. Those buried yearnings had been briefly revived, only to be smothered, and now she felt as if she
was moving not towards an elusive dream but an inexor-
able destiny bound up with Edward Lockwood. She had
tried, she thought, to explain about him to Lindsay, but
fate seemed to have willed it otherwise, preventing the

explanation and leaving the Resident convinced that she had been false.

She was roused from these grey reveries by the brisk voice of Pannabai, who brought in tea and fruit juice, beaming.

'You must be down by nine o'clock, Miss Saheb. The wedding starts then.'

'I shall be ready, Pannabai,' Caroline assured her.

'The Maharani has asked me to dress you,' the maid-servant said, setting down Caroline's breakfast.

'I can manage . . . I need help only with my hair,' Caroline said.

'Ah! But today I dress you differently,' Pannabai explained. Having prepared the cool scented bath, Pannabai disappeared, while Caroline luxuriated in the refreshing water, and returned carrying a long tissue-wrapped box. Chunibai followed with a small jewel-box and a tray of flowers.

'What is all this?' Caroline asked, wide-eyed.

'Aha! You will soon see. Chunibai and I are to dress you in the Hindu manner!'

Caroline wrapped a towel round her, and stepped out of the bathtub. 'Who sent all this?'

'The Maharani. Why, don't you like them?' Pannabai asked sharply.

'They're beautiful!'

'Specially ordered from Benares for you, Miss Saheb,' Chunibai murmured timidly.

Caroline was dressed amid sighs and cries of admiration from her maids. They then led her to the marquee on the lawn, erected for the wedding. Shyly, she went up to the Maharani to thank her for the finery.

Sitadevi touched Caroline's cheeks, and said, 'How

lovely you look, my dear. I would not have thought a woman with your European colouring would look so exquisite in a sari.'

'The girl has fine features,' the Maharaja's third wife conceded.

'Sit down, my dear,' Sitadevi said. 'Padmini wants you to be near her during the wedding. Ah, there comes Sir Julian. I shall ask him to join us.'

Caroline turned, despite her resolve not to do so. Lindsay stood before her, in morning dress, looking grave and distinguished. His brilliant blue eyes surveyed Caroline slowly as she stood in an emerald green sari embroidered with gold thread. Far from concealing her figure, its folds seemed to emphasise the curves of her breast and hips, revealing a firm smooth midriff and round slim arms. Gold filigee jewellery adorned her neck, wrists and ears. A golden chain twined in her hair, which had been gathered into a chignon at her neck. A vermilion *bindi* gleamed on her smooth forehead. Freed from the stiff, voluminous crinoline, Caroline looked sensuous and supple in the sari. Only her eyes, normally jewel-bright, were shadowed by an unspoken sadness as she saw her dreams fade.

'I did not recognise you,' Lindsay murmured, his gaze fixed on her, his mind agitated by a hundred inconsequential thoughts.

'Nor I you,' she murmured back, unable to tear her gaze from his face, also touched by a strange wistfulness.

'Perhaps you are two Rajputs separated in your last life and destined to be united here,' the Maharani's soft voice intoned, weaving a momentary spell between Sir Julian and Caroline, but it was her voice again which dissolved the magic. 'But why don't you sit down, Your Excellency? Kamal wants you to be near, as you have been a friend and brother to him. You too, Caroline,' she added gently.

He was about to sit down, when he saw Edward emerging onto the lawn. At once his face hardened, as he asked an attendant grimly, 'Bring Lockwood Saheb here.'

Caroline felt as she had been thrusted back to reality again. Behind the Honourable Edward Lockwood came Lydia Dalrymple and her mother. She shrank back against one of the royal concubines, hoping that Edward and the Dalrymple ladies would not see her.

Edward, however, sighted her at once and after a moment of visible confusion said clearly, 'Who—Caro! I wouldn't have recognised you! What have you done to yourself?'

Caroline winced, and put a finger on her lips to silence him as he sat next to the Resident, whose sardonic expression did nothing to alleviate her distress.

'Miss Emerson looks very exotic,' he remarked dryly.

'Quite!' Edward agreed. 'Whatever possessed you to dress like this, Caro?' He then turned to Lindsay. 'Is this customary, Sir Julian?'

'No, Lockwood,' he replied coldly. 'But it is a gesture of courtesy.'

'Oh . . . yes,' Edward muttered, sinking into the cushioned seat with evident perplexity, but his expression lightened when he saw Lydia Dalrymple smile brightly at him. He could not help wishing that Caroline could be more like her.

A burst of shehnai playing the *Multani* raga announced the advent of the two bridegrooms followed by the two Maharajas and other kinsmen. They made a brilliant procession in their brocade *shervanis*, silk *churidars* and turbans as they walked slowly from the palace veranda to the canopied square where the sacred fire was already burning. Then as the shehnai softened into *Thumree*, the tinkle of many bells heralded the coming of the two brides. The two Maharanis came towards them, and performed *aroti* by walking with lamps round the brides, who sat next to their fathers facing the bridegrooms.

The shehnai and tabla fell silent, and the priests began to intone Sanskrit verses invoking the blessings of the gods of fire, earth, wind, sky and water. Lindsay closed his eyes, remembering how long ago he had read these immortal verses from the *Rig Veda*, the poems composed by the ancient Aryans when they had first settled in north India. The priests went on reciting and chanting the three-thousand-year-old verses of the marriage ceremony as each ritual was performed. First the fathers gave the brides away to the bridegrooms. Then the young couples stood up and walked seven times round the sacred fire, vowing to love and protect each other. Afterwards, they sat together while the parents sat apart, their task completed. The priests threw clarified butter onto the sandalwood logs and, as the flames leapt upwards, more Sanskrit verses were chanted, uniting the couples in the presence of the elemental witnesses-fire, water, earth and air.

Quietly Lindsay explained the meaning of the verses to Caroline and Edward, and in the process revealed to them a little of the ancient heritage of India.

Prince Kamal and Prince Uday stood up, as did their brides, and together they bent down to touch the feet of the four parents standing close together. Then the Maharani of Vijaypur stepped forward and showered rose petals on them. Others followed suit. Conch shells were blown to drive away evil spirits. When everyone pressed forward to greet the newly-wed couples, the shehnai and tabla began a flirtation with each other, filling the warm April with a gay raga.

Lindsay stood back while the Rajput chiefs greeted the newly-weds, with Caroline, exotic and lovely, beside him; both under the spell of the beautiful marriage ceremony.

A grand luncheon for the guests was served on the long veranda of the palace. The brides broke their long fast with aromatic vegetables, saffron-scented meats, rice cooked with raisins and almonds, sweets encrusted with beaten silver and iced fruits. Outside, in the canopied square, the less exalted visitors of Vijaypur were served the same delicious food with greater gusto and less formality.

When luncheon was over, Caroline walked towards the lakeside and stood under a scarlet Flame of the Forest, staring pensively at Lotus Mahal, forlorn and weary.

After chatting with the pretty Lydia, Edward went in search of Caroline and found her by the water's edge. 'Well, Caro, that's that! Now that these weddings are over, we can think of ours,' he said eagerly.

'What is the hurry?' she mumbled, trying to stave off the inevitable event.

'Hurry?' Edward echoed. 'The P & O liner sails from Bombay in ten days! If we are to marry, travel, and get some proper clothes for you in Bombay, it will take time.'

'Ten days?' she whispered. 'That's all?' Panic tied knots of apprehension in her stomach.

He smiled. 'Is it too long to wait, Caro? Of course we can have a little honeymoon here before we leave for Bombay. That little villa on the lake—that should do. As a matter of fact, Caro, I asked Lindsay if we might use it until our departure.'

'You . . . asked him?' she exclaimed in a strangled voice.

'Couldn't very well ask the Maharaja, you know,' Edward replied blandly.

Caroline looked so stricken that Edward asked, 'What's the matter, Caro, don't you like the place?'

She stared at Lotus Mahal floating on the sunlit waters of Lake Rashmi, remembering the night of Holi. 'What did . . . Sir Julian . . . say?'

Edward shrugged. 'Didn't disagree exactly, but didn't sound over-enthusiastic either. Seems to have a dislike of the place. Are there ghosts there?'

A sob was wrenched from Caroline, churning up the suppressed agony of the last twenty-four hours. Covering her face with her hands, she broke into convulsive sobbing.

Edward watched her in utter bewilderment and then put his arms around her. He was surprised still more when she remained stiff and unyielding in his embrace, her hands covering her face as she wept in sheer abandon. For a while he held her, and then released her, unable to understand the cause of such stormy emotions.

From afar, Lindsay, on his way back to the Residency, saw Caroline standing in the circle of Edward's arms. He did not see her tears or hear her cry. All he could see was her shimmering green figure, sunlight glinting on her auburn hair, and the scarlet blossoms of the Flame of the Forest blazing in the afternoon sunlight. For a moment, the bright afternoon turned suddenly dark. It was as if his worst fears and doubts about her had been confirmed.

Angrily he shook himself free of that brief and aching sensation.

By the water's edge, Caroline's tears subsided, and she became aware of Edward's eyes on her. 'It's the infernal heat,' he said, looking at her. 'It does strange things to people. Why don't you go in and rest?'

She nodded, suddenly embarrassed by her outburst, and made a move to go. Troubled by her expression, he detained her. 'Caro, you will marry me soon, won't you?'

'Do you really want me to?' she said in a flat, toneless voice.

'I do wish it. Always have,' Edward said quietly.

'I seem to remember a time when you . . . changed your mind after papa . . .' Caroline's dull voice hardened, as did her tear-rimmed eyes.

He sighed. 'I've hated myself for what happened. I came to India after my work in Alexandria was over—to look for you. In Calcutta, you gave me no opportunity to declare myself.'

'And you were preparing to return to England without . . . expressing your sentiments!' Caroline retorted.

'I was planning to pass through Vijaypur en route to Bombay . . . Believe me!'

There was a boyish entreaty in the young man's voice as he stood there in a heavy dark suit, his fair hair bleached by the cruel sun, grey eyes almost transparent in the relentless light. Caroline's heart contracted with an infuriating mixture of impatience and compassion.

'I believe you,' she said, sighing.

His smile was one of relief. 'I'm so glad. Shall we go back? I believe the Dalrymples are giving a reception in honour of the newly-weds tonight. We can dance, too.

Do you remember the ball, Caro, when I first proposed to you?'

She nodded as the memory brought back remembrances of her father and their misfortune.

'Tonight I shall ask you again on bended knees,' he said, raising her hand to his lips. 'And tomorrow . . . or the next day . . . we shall be married by the Reverend Archibald Palgrave. Does that please you, my lady?'

'Immensely,' Caroline replied in a tight, barely controlled, voice.

'Good,' he said, pressing her hand to his heart as they made their way back to their rooms.

Vijaypur palace looked like a glittering jewel that evening as lamps burned in every window, on terrace balustrades, cornices and pillars. Huge lanterns of coloured glass hung over doors. Guests in shimmering silks, brocades and flashing jewels thronged the lawns, where wine and champagne flowed as freely as the fountains. The shehnai and tabla of the morning were replaced by a military band which played Strauss waltzes. The scent of jasmine and tuberoses was all-pervasive.

The two princes and their brides walked slowly, stopping to talk with guests on receiving their congratulations. Princess Indumati was a shy girl of sixteen, unaccustomed to the socialising expected by her husband. He had insisted that she should not observe purdah and should mix freely with Vijaypuris. As a concession to custom, he allowed her to drape the *anchal* of her sari half over her head, so that everyone could see the fresh face and the diffident smile. Princess Padmini was radiant and vibrant as she walked beside Prince Uday of Tewar. The Maharajas of Vijaypur and Tewar sat on gilded chairs, looking as unlike as possible.

Caroline was at hand to help the Maharani with the lady guests, who were sitting clustered together, their faces veiled. She watched Lindsay move among the visitors with an air of friendly dignity. When dinner was served, there was considerable movement as people thronged the tables.

After dinner the young people drove away to attend the party given by Colonel and Mrs Dalrymple, passing along the poplar-lined drive illuminated by earthenware lamps until they were going by open fields under a dark sky embroidered, it seemed, by a billion stars.

Caroline sat in the carriage with Princess Padmini, who had insisted on her accompanying them—putting an end to Edward's arguments that he should escort Caroline.

'Is it true, Miss Caroline?' the Princess asked in a hushed tone.

'Is what true, Princess?' Caroline asked wearily.

'That you will be leaving Vijaypur in a few days to return to England as Mrs Lockwood?' Caroline did not reply, but the irrepressible Princess went on. 'I would not have guessed that your heart lay there.'

'Can we always follow our hearts? Do we not seek the safe harbour instead of stormy seas?' Caroline murmured. Padmini clasped her hand and, even in the lamplit carriage, Caroline saw the entreaty in the young bride's face to drop such a perilous topic. Richard Brooke had been an uncharted sea from which the Princess had retreated.

The rest of the drive was accomplished in silence until they drove up to the portico of the commanding officer's rambling bungalow. Barouches and carriages arrived, disgorging passengers before trundling into the main courtyard.

Edward was waiting to escort Caroline to the entrance hall where crinolines billowed out like full-blown flowers mingling with the shimmer of a few saris. All the men wore western evening dress. The guests were presented to the two princes and their brides. Princess Padmini took her shy sister-in-law in hand, and encouraged her to speak to the English ladies in halting English, but Caroline noticed that Princess Indumati tired easily and soon sat down. Lydia Dalrymple, dressed virginally in white taffeta, watched Caroline with a triumphant smile. She had sensed that the Resident was no longer interested in the governess, and rejoiced in that knowledge.

Shortly afterwards, dancing began as the Vijaypur Lancers band struck up waltzes and mazurkas. Edward wasted no time in leading Caroline to the dance-floor. She followed, silent and unresisting, remembering the last time she had danced with Edward almost three years ago, when her world had been unclouded by disasters.

'Perhaps he remembers it, too,' Caroline thought grimly, and wondered if he had come to make amends. She was sitting by herself, still wrapped in thoughts of the past, when Julian Lindsay came to ask her for a dance.

Calmly, with every sign of polite indifference, Caroline accepted the invitation, allowing him to lead her on to the floor. It was one thing to feign indifference; it was another to feel his gloved right hand on her waist, their free hands interlaced as they swirled together to the tune of 'Vienna Woods'. She tried to rivet her eyes to his shirt-front, but her gaze invariably moved up to find him contemplating her with unnerving intensity. Memories lapsed in the turmoil of the present, as Caroline was aware of a desperate longing still undefeated by the hauteur of the face above her.

When the music stopped, he bowed. 'Thank you, Miss Emerson, for our second and last dance together.'

Caroline felt her desperate hopes crushed by his tone. She inclined her head in acknowledgment and then, eyes burning, walked slowly back to Edward, with whom Lydia was flirting demurely. For his part, he seemed to be more at ease with her than with the unpredictable Caroline.

'I have been exchanging impressions with Mr Lockwood,' Lydia said sweetly. 'We do seem to concur on so many matters, do we not?'

'Oh, most definitely. I find the Resident so difficult to understand,' he complained.

'Yes, he has the oddest notions about . . .' Seeing the surprise on Caroline's face, Lydia checked herself on time.

'You take good care to conceal your views before the Resident,' Caroline said softly to the younger girl, and walked away, wondering why she should defend him after the cold manner in which he treated her.

The evening dragged on. Supper was eaten, and the music began again. Edward began dancing with Miss Dalrymple, apparently relieved to be freed from the necessity of enduring Caroline's inexplicable mood. Caroline slipped away unseen to the quiet garden for a breath of air. She sat there, heedless of the passage of time, of how the warm April air had suddenly become cool. Trees rustled in the breeze, dry leaves crackled. She was aware of a desolation deepening within her as she sat in a shadowy part of the garden, where an old banyan tree spread its many gnarled branches. The sound of footsteps over the leaves caused her to turn.

Lindsay stood in the shadows.

'I came to say goodbye, Miss Emerson,' he said in a low voice.

Caroline tried to speak, but no sound came from her throat.

'I believe you will be leaving in two days for Bombay. I may not be able to attend your . . . wedding. I shall be accompanying the Maharaja to Jaipur, where we have urgent business,' he said hurriedly.

She nodded, finding it impossible to speak. Then, unable to endure the thought of not seeing him again, she rose and made a move to go. At once he stepped forward, and, with a violence she had never suspected of him, seized her shoulders.

'Where are you going?' he asked, teeth clenched.

'To . . . the house,' she whispered, trembling from head to toe.

'Why? Will it ruin your reputation to be seen alone with me here?'

Caroline stared at him incredulously.

'You ought not to worry about your reputation any more, Miss Emerson, because you will soon be safely ensconced in Society as the future Countess of Elverston. But, until then, why not tarry a while here? After all, you were prepared to stand in full view of hundreds of wedding guests in the arms of your . . . fiancé!'

Caroline found her voice at last. 'It was not as you think . . . Believe me . . .' she began, when he interposed with suppressed violence.

'I shall never believe you! Never! Do you understand? You are the most feckless and despicable woman I know. How you have fooled me! I, who judged myself to be a discerning man! Who would guess from the innocence of your eyes that your lips could be so false?'

Caroline was terrified by the passion on his face and in his voice. His hands pressed her shoulders painfully. His eyes glittered with an inner fury.

'But, before I let you leave, Miss Emerson, I want a last taste of your sweet and treacherous lips!'

'No!' she cried brokenly, at breaking point. 'Please . . .' Her words were smothered by Julian's lips. There was no tenderness in them as they possessed hers. He rained kisses on her lips, neck and cheeks; burning, bruising kisses that held no gentleness. When Caroline resisted, his fury only increased, for he crushed her in his arms until she cried out in anguish. 'Please! I beg you! You have hurt me enough . . . More than anyone else in the world!'

The broken voice seemed to bring Julian back to his senses. He released her abruptly, so that she staggered, and almost fell against the banyan tree. She steadied herself, gasping for breath.

'Go back now, Miss Emerson,' the Resident of Vijaypur said with barely-concealed hatred. 'You don't belong here. You belong to Lockwood and to his world . . . of bright lights, intrigues and idle chatter. What folly made me think you had a mind worth discovering, a heart worth winning, you contemptible gadfly!'

Trembling with rage, Caroline stood up and met his burning gaze. 'I intend to do just that, Sir Julian! I have yearned to return to my own world. Edward will treat me with far greater kindness and respect than you are capable of doing. I shall be happy with him in that world which you so despise. What woman could you please— you utterly self-centred man! I, too, am sorry for having met you, and despise myself for believing that you were a man of vision and originality. You are a man who craves only dominion over others—as ruthless and arbitrary as any adventurer of the East India Company who bled this wretched country white!'

She was quivering like a leaf as she finished speaking. Lindsay watched her in anguished silence. Unable to stand it any more, Caroline picked up her skirts and ran, never once turning to look back to where he sat, hands over his eyes in an attitude of total defeat.

CHAPTER
FIFTEEN

THE SUN was high overhead when Caroline awoke from a fitful sleep, exhausted from the previous night's trauma. The tea had cooled next to her and a dry gritty breeze blew in through the windows. She dreaded facing the day and debated whether she should coax herself back to sleep, but memories of the previous evening drove away all thoughts of repose.

'It's a nightmare,' she told herself, 'and I shall wake up to find it unreal. He cannot possibly hate me so much! How have I been false and treacherous? It is not I who encouraged him. It is he who led me to believe in foolish dreams by his moments of tenderness.'

Tears streamed down her cheeks at the thought of those brief encounters with him when her heart had soared to the sky in joy, when he had held out the promise of happiness. 'Was it my imagination only, or did he really care for me? But if he did, the arrival of Edward Lockwood would not have deterred him. And now I must go away as the wife of Edward.'

Caroline buried her face in the lace-trimmed pillows and wept. Gradually, as her tears subsided, she wondered why Pannabai had not come to help her to dress or brought water to the bathroom next door. Why, for that matter, was the palace so silent? Had not the Maharaja's family planned the post-nuptial ceremonies for this morning?

Slowly, with an instinctive sense of trouble, Caroline went to the bathroom and found that the tub had been half-filled with water, and toilet articles were scattered around, as though Pannabai had been hastily summoned elsewhere. She filled the tub, bathed and dressed hastily, then went towards the Maharani's apartment in the next wing.

There, a strange sight greeted her. Princess Padmini was weeping outside the door, as a wan-faced Prince Kamal and Lindsay stood talking to Dr Williams. With a thudding heart Caroline went over to them, past a corridor lined with frightened retainers.

'What has happened?' she asked the Resident quietly.

He was himself again—calm, and totally in command. There was not a tiny residue showing of the previous night's violent emotions. 'It might, for all I know, have been someone else,' Caroline thought.

'The Maharaja has been ill since last night. The Maharani, too, is showing the same symptoms. Dr Williams thinks it might be typhoid.' He spoke with an impersonal civility. Caroline stifled a shiver of apprehension. 'How did they contract it? We are all so careful here!'

Lindsay frowned. 'I, too, am puzzled. For several years there have not been any epidemics here . . . unless one of the guests from Tewar brought the infection.'

Prince Kamal looked troubled. 'Let us not lay blame at anyone's door. If we insult the Maharaja of Tewar, the fate of my sister will be bleak indeed,' he said, glancing at Princess Padmini weeping by the door, still dressed in the traditional pink sari of a wedding.

Padmini ceased to weep, and cried in a hoarse voice, 'I

will not go to Tewar! I will not leave my mother!' In a flash she was turning the handle of the Maharani's door. Lindsay caught both her arms and held her back. 'My child,' he said in a unusually gentle voice, 'you are now the second lady of Tewar. The Maharaja has no son. Your husband is next in line and will need you by his side. You must not endanger yourself. Prepare to leave immediately!'

Prince Uday Singh emerged out of the crowd, pushing his way to his young bride. 'No one,' he said grimly, glancing at Prince Kamal, 'shall hurt your sister as long as I am alive.' He took his wife from the Resident's clasp, and held her firmly. 'I shall tell my brother, the Maharaja of Tewar, that we must leave this morning.'

'Thank you, Your Highness,' the Resident said. He turned to Dr Williams. 'Tell us exactly what you want done. I have already instructed the Lancers to take the necessary precautions.' His glance strayed to Caroline, who was standing by a window, staring at the deserted, sunlit gardens which only yesterday had been the scene of festivities and merriment. For a time he seemed lost in thought as he watched her still figure. It was as though both were now becalmed after yesterday's tempests.

'Miss Emerson?' he finally called.

Caroline turned round, 'Yes, Sir Julian?'

'Please meet me in the sitting-room in the west wing. I have something important to tell you.'

'Can you not tell me here?'

He gave her a rueful smile. 'Don't be afraid of any more . . . untoward incidents, Miss Emerson. There will be none. I shall see you downstairs in ten minutes, after I have finished talking to Dr Williams.'

Caroline approached the closed door of the

Maharani's room. Dr Williams glanced at her over his half-moon glasses, and then looked at the Resident.

'What is it, Miss Emerson? Why don't you go down?' Lindsay asked.

'I wish to see the Maharani.'

'I am afraid, miss, that's impossible,' the doctor said firmly.

'It is quite possible, Doctor. You have only to open the door and allow me to pass,' Caroline retorted.

'We cannot risk your contracting the infection, Miss Emerson,' the Resident declared. 'Go down, if you please.'

Hiding her frustration, Caroline went downstairs to wait in the cool sitting-room where the Maharaja usually met the Resident to discuss state affairs. Outside, the Flame of the Forest bloomed in a blaze of scarlet and, further down the garden, plump yellow mangoes were ripening. A sweet, heavy, smell pervaded the place.

Presently Lindsay entered the room, immaculate in a light linen suit. His clean-shaven tanned face and neatly brushed dark hair gave no indication of the fact that he had been roused before dawn by an anxious Prince Kamal, who came to tell him that his parents were seriously ill. Only the dark shadows round his eyes and the lines round his mouth betrayed his weariness.

'Miss Emerson,' he said, indicating that she should sit, and taking a chair at some distance from her. 'I have informed Edward Lockwood about the situation here.'

'What does he say?'

'He wants to leave Vijaypur immediately.' Lindsay paused. 'Before he can leave with you, it is necessary of course that . . . you are married.' He faltered, as if the subject were distasteful.

Caroline felt her cheeks burning, and averted her eyes.

'Unfortunately, the local vicar is away just now. I've sent word for him to be here by this afternoon. Will you be ready by then for your wedding?'

Caroline nodded. 'You will be here? You cannot possibly be going to Jaipur now?'

'Yes, I shall be here, Miss Emerson,' he said grimly. 'If it will make you any happier, I shall be present at your wedding.'

Caroline rose abruptly. 'That is entirely up to you, Sir Julian,' she said quietly and, dropping a perfunctory curtsy, hastened out of the room. The Resident continued to sit for a while, staring out of the window, and then roused himself to face the situation.

Meanwhile Caroline sped towards her room. The palace was now filled with silent figures moving soundlessly, as if waiting for a disaster.

'Today! I am to be married today,' she thought, as panic rose within her, wiping out all other thoughts but that single stark one. She was to be married to the Honourable Edward Lockwood, who was likely to be the future Earl of Elverston, the fair, grey-eyed Adonis of her girlhood who had once caused her such unhappiness. She might one day become the Countess of Elverston, a respected member of high society. How pleased Aunt Hester would be to hear the news! 'But papa?' she thought suddenly. 'Would papa like this?' She brushed aside her doubts. 'I shall marry him . . . and try to be happy,' she promised herself.

Later in the morning, Padmini came to bid farewell. 'What a way to begin a new life,' she cried, throwing herself into Caroline's gentle arms.

'Hush, my dear! All will be well,' Caroline comforted the distraught young bride.

'What if mother dies? Oh, Miss Caroline, what shall I do?' Caroline stroked the dark head close to her. 'She will recover, my dear. I promise you.'

The Princess looked at Caroline with glittering eyes. 'You will look after mother, won't you? You are sensible, and seem to know something about medicines.'

Caroline's fingers ceased to stroke the silky head. 'You want me to stay here, Padmini?' she asked in a serious tone.

'You will not desert us all now? Mother needs you . . . and so does Kamal's new bride. How can you go now?'

Caroline sighed, distressed.

A servant came to call Padmini, as the Tewar guests were ready to leave. The two young women clung to each other for reassurance, and then the new bride half-ran from the room in a flood of tears.

Caroline busied herself with her packing, glancing at dresses which had happy memories. Pannabai sniffed, and Chunibai murmured lamentations on Miss Saheb's departure. By the afternoon, Caroline's nerves were taut with anxiety. Several times she had sent Chunibai to find out if the Padre sahib had returned, and was eventually told that he had reached the Residency.

Caroline walked slowly down the stairs and through the corridors to the garden. A coral twilight was giving way to a purple dusk as she strode purposefully towards the Residency where Edward Lockwood and the Reverend Mr Palgrave awaited her.

There was a flurry among the retainers as she entered, and if they were surprised to see her in a simple muslin dress, they concealed it, unlike her three countrymen.

'Why aren't you dressed yet, Caro?' Edward asked in exasperation. 'We must leave soon!'

The vicar shook his head at feminine vagary, but the Resident, who had been sitting in a corner of the veranda outside, smoking moodily, hastened to the drawing-room to survey the situation. An ironic smile temporarily lit his face as he watched Edward's annoyance and Caroline's unconcern.

'Hardly the dress for a future Countess,' Lindsay murmured.

She looked at him, and nodded. 'I quite agree, Sir Julian. But this is not my wedding dress.'

'Where is your wedding dress, then?' Edward asked in an irate voice.

'I haven't the vaguest notion, Edward. It must be still a twinkle in my dressmaker's eye,' Caroline replied sweetly.

'Caroline!' Edward thundered, out of all patience. 'For heaven's sake, come to your senses! We must be off as soon as the vicar has performed the ceremony!'

'There will be no ceremony,' she announced softly.

A shocked silence greeted her words. The vicar groaned: had he been summoned to hasten to the city, over dusty village tracks, only for this?

Edward strode up to her and shouted, 'Look, Caro, stop all this nonsense! It is a matter of our safety. Come, Mr Palgrave, get out your books,' he said, half-dragging Caroline towards the weary vicar.

She turned to glance at the Resident, who was frowning thoughtfully, and then said in a matter-of-fact tone, 'I would be delighted to complete the formalities, Edward, but it would be unfair of me not to warn you that I am likely to be the next victim after the Maharani.'

Two voices cried out in horror and dismay as their

owners stepped back instinctively. Lindsay was silent, but he paled visibly. Then he asked sharply, 'How do you know?'

'I was continuously with Her Highness these last few days,' she replied slowly, and placed a pale hand on her forehead. 'I also feel strange . . . hot and dry.' Turning to a horrified Lockwood, she said, 'Do you understand now, Edward, why I am dressed like this? You had better carry on, and if God wills I shall join you in England at the earliest.'

Lindsay left the room, and stood outside in the dusk to allow the lovers some privacy to make their plans. A strange fear clutched at him, weakening all his resolve.

With a visible effort, he mastered himself and then returned to the room. 'Lockwood,' he said firmly, 'you cannot leave Miss Emerson behind. I suggest you wait for a few days . . . the temperature may be due to a touch of the sun. If she does not show symptoms within that time, you can proceed with your original plans.'

'But the P & O liner sails in eight days!' Edward protested.

'Three days to wait here, three days to travel to Bombay . . . that should be quite enough. You will not be able to enjoy a little honeymoon at Lotus Mahal . . . but that can't be helped.' Lindsay glanced at Caroline as he finished. She remained impassive, as though Lotus Mahal had no significance any more.

Edward reluctantly agreed. Mr Palgrave blew out his cheeks in patient exasperation. Caroline went to the open door leading to the veranda. 'May I take leave of you, gentlemen? I feel I need to rest.'

'Take care, Caro,' Edward said, approaching her with some trepidation.

'Yes, Miss Emerson, take care of yourself,' Lindsay echoed him. 'Typhoid is very dangerous.'

If Caroline was offended by the Resident's odd tone, she did not show it. 'He is, we all know, an unfeeling soul,' she thought, brushing away the anger that swelled within her at his cold attitude to her predicament. 'Or has he guessed that I am pretending to be sick? Does he know that ginger tea can raise the body temperature?' She chuckled in amusement at the thought of fooling them all with her ruse to stay on in Vijaypur.

In the evening she went to the Maharani, when no one was present to prevent her from entering. She advanced slowly, fearfully, into the darkened room where the invalid lay on a huge bed, flushed and exhausted.

'My child,' Sitadevi murmured, her red-rimmed eyes fixed on Caroline. 'You ought not to have come. If you fall ill, how will you make the journey to England?'

'Hush, Your Highness! I am strong, and shall look after you . . . as I promised Padmini I would.'

The Maharani closed her eyes. She was beyond argument with the self-willed governess, but the touch of cool hands sponging her face, arms and shoulders, the taste of iced lemonade on her parched lips were very welcome. Unresistingly, she allowed Caroline to nurse her.

'Where did you learn to look after the sick, child?' she enquired weakly.

'Downstairs—in Dr Williams's waiting-room!' Caroline said softly.

'He allowed you to come?'

'He was happy to have help.'

When Sitadevi had fallen into a heavy slumber,

Caroline, exhausted since the day before, dozed in a deep chair.

For two days Caroline helped Dr Williams with the Maharani, and with the assistance of the retainers managed to slip away before her presence could be detected by either Prince Kamal or the Resident, who believed her to be resting in her room.

On the third day, however, she allowed herself to be discovered in the Maharani's room. It had been decided that if she did not develop symptoms of typhoid by then, she would leave with Edward. She watched Prince Kamal and the Resident as they entered, and was delighted by the stunned expression on their faces.

'What are you doing here?' Lindsay demanded harshly, advancing towards her.

'What I have been doing for three days—nursing the Maharani,' Caroline said demurely.

'Three days! You have been coming here for three days?' The Prince was incredulous.

'Yes, Your Highness.'

Lindsay looked closely at her. 'Were you not supposed to be resting, as you developed a fever on the eve of your wedding?'

Caroline could not meet the piercing look of his eyes, and her rising colour betrayed her.

'It was a ruse, was it not, Miss Emerson?'

'If you wish to put it that way,' she retorted. 'But my reason was that I had promised Princess Padmini to stay and look after her mother.'

'Padmini had no right to ask such a sacrifice of you,' Prince Kamal cried. 'And you had no obligation to agree.'

Caroline was silent. The Resident regarded her keenly. 'Why did you do it, Miss Emerson?'

'Padmini had such touching faith in western medicine that she felt my presence was a guarantee of the Maharani's recovery. I could not fail her.' Her eyes twinkled with gentle malice. 'And it would not reflect well on the British Raj if an English governess ran away at the first sign of trouble!'

The Prince laughed. 'Pardon me, if I say that you are incorrigible!' He grew serious instantly, however. 'But, Miss Emerson, what if you do fall ill?'

Filled with a reluctant esteem for her nonchalant behaviour, Lindsay had been watching her closely. 'But then,' he thought, 'she has always has been unpredictable!' Aloud, he said, 'Before you do fall ill, Miss Emerson, I shall see that you leave today for Bombay. Everything is prepared.'

The impersonal coolness of his tone checked Caroline's exuberance and made her pause. 'I shall not go just now, Your Excellency,' she said in a determined manner. 'I have been exposed to the infection, and would not dream of infecting Edward. I may be one of those fortunate people who do not catch typhoid, but we do not know about him.'

Lindsay regarded her with an impassive face, but behind the imperturbable façade Caroline fancied she saw a chaos of emotions firmly subdued. 'I doubt if Edward Lockwood will leave without you,' he said quietly.

'Then he must stay . . . until the situation improves.'

The Resident nodded, and then Dr Williams came in to assure them that the Maharani was fighting the disease. 'I dare say Miss Emerson's very presence makes a difference. The Maharaja is not resisting so well, I fear.'

'Are there any more cases of typhoid? In the town or surrounding villages?' Prince Kamal asked.

'Not yet, but . . .' Dr Williams seemed troubled. 'I came to tell you that I suspect that Princess Indumati might be coming down with the infection.'

'No!' the Prince whispered. 'How can that be?'

'I am afraid so, Your Highness. In fact I saw her just now. She has a high temperature and . . . begged me to warn you to stay away.'

But Kamal had already left the room and was heard running over the marble floors to the east wing where he shared an apartment with his new bride.

'How sick is she?' the Resident asked.

Dr Williams sighed. 'Who can say? It all depends on her powers of resistance.'

'I saw Princess Indumati looking tired and listless at the Dalrymples' party,' Caroline recalled, and then looked away, remembering that night's encounter with the Resident.

'We shall need more medicines, Sir Julian,' the doctor said. 'Perhaps you could send someone to Ajmer? It's a big cantonment town and bound to stock all we require.'

'It shall be done,' he assured him. 'I shall get a message to the commanding officer, and ask if the Lancers can go at all speed.'

Before leaving, Lindsay had another word with Caroline. 'You are quite certain you wish to stay on? I fear that the disease will spread. You must think clearly of the possible consequences, Miss Emerson.'

'I have no choice, Sir Julian. If I went away, I could endanger others, since I have been exposed to the infection.'

He sighed, and Caroline thought that, for once, he made no attempt to conceal his deep anxiety.

'Very well. Good day. I shall tell Lockwood of your decision.'

Despite everyone's expectation that the typhoid would spread, it did not. Only the Maharaja, the Maharani and Prince Kamal's bride showed evidence of illness. Dr Williams was puzzled, and relieved that the dread fever had not spread to the town and countryside.

The Resident, too, was puzzled, and discussed the matter with the doctor. 'What could it have been that caused their illness?' he asked. 'A common source of food and water would have affected others, but it has not. Could they have eaten something that the others did not?'

The doctor met the Resident's gaze over his half-glasses. 'What are you saying, Your Excellency? That those three people have been deliberately . . . poisoned?' His voice faltered.

Lindsay sighed and nodded his head. 'It is possible, is it not, Doctor?'

'I . . . suppose it is. But who . . . ?'

'I cannot be certain, but can guess.' He paused. 'You will warn the Prince . . . about food and drink? He may be the next victim.'

Dr Williams promised to take all possible precautions, and to advise Prince Kamal and also Caroline.

During the next week, Caroline helped to nurse the Maharani and Princess Indumati. Dr Williams praised her competence to the Resident. 'She has no feminine flutterings, no exhibition of nerves, no display of a natural shrinking from sickness.'

Lindsay listened, feeling an inexplicable sadness. Sensing that the doctor was watching him curiously, he said, 'Such qualities will help her, no doubt, in her future rôle.'

Since Dr Williams, like everyone in Vijaypur, did not know of Edward Lockwood's plan to marry Caroline, he was puzzled, but did not press further, and once more expressed his gratitude that Miss Emerson was at hand to help in the crisis.

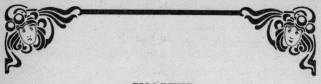

CHAPTER
SIXTEEN

THE SUMMER sun blazed relentlessly, turning leaves to cinder, drying up streams and lakes, until only the cracked brown earth dominated the landscape. The deep blue sky was cloudless, with no hint of rain to relieve the parched world.

Caroline stood on a balcony one late afternoon in May, scanning the harsh scenery before her. 'There is something cruel and sinister about this season,' she thought with a shudder despite the heat that enveloped her. The heat had, however, destroyed diseases as well. The typhoid victims had survived, thanks to timely action and because Dr Williams had ensured that the contagion had been contained. But the Maharaja, weakened by a life of dissipation, was visibly sinking. The chief Maharani, whom he had humiliated by taking concubines, was the only wife who went to sit at his side, despite her own weakened condition. Returning to her room, Sitadevi would pray that the life of her husband might be spared.

Watching her, Caroline wondered at the strength of her devotion, which had survived despite the lack of reciprocity and tacit rejection. She wondered if she could have forgiven so many transgressions, while rebuking herself for thinking ill of a man who was ill. Already there was that hushed, almost reverential, atmosphere that surrounds the death of an exalted person.

The Maharaja's condition had already raised various problems. His Council of Ministers and the Resident agreed that Crown Prince Kamal should discharge the Maharaja's duties, and he turned to his friend and mentor, the Resident, for advice in complicated matters. This development created some uneasiness among the more orthodox ministers, who feared that the Prince, influenced by the Englishman, would introduce changes and customs that were common enough in modernised Calcutta but anathema in feudal Rajputana. There were already murmurs of doubt and dissent against the Crown Prince among the older advisers of his father.

Lindsay's close involvement in state matters left him little time to entertain his reluctant guest, the Honourable Edward Lockwood, who refused to stir beyond the walls of the Residency for fear of falling ill. Caroline was forced to visit him and hear his acerbic comments on his host. She wondered whether Edward's enforced stay in Vijaypur had stimulated his lively dislike of Lindsay, or whether he had guessed her feelings towards the Resident.

One day, when Edward criticised Lindsay for 'burying himself in benighted places and indulging in oriental intrigues', Caroline lost her patience and defended the Resident warmly. Edward, glanced at her quizzically. 'You are beginning to sound like Lindsay,' he said in a carping voice.

She lowered her eyes, fearful of betraying herself, but Edward continued in a disapproving tone. 'I can only hope you will change, when you are back in your own environment and take your proper place in society.'

'What if I don't change, Edward?' There was a rebellious spark in her eyes.

'You will cause much unhappiness all round,' he replied calmly. 'I trust you do want to be happy?'

Caroline had turned from him, trying to gather courage to confess her predicament. For the first time, Edward wondered why she had become so different. A shadow of doubt crossed his mind. 'Can it be that she doesn't care?' he asked himself, but the idea seemed ridiculous, and he dismissed it. An uneasiness remained in his mind, however. Sensing this, she stayed away, wondering how she could solve her terrible predicament.

Standing on the balcony adjoining her room, Caroline decided to go for a ride, hoping that the outing would clear her head. The hot sun had dipped over the orange-rimmed horizon when she set off for Devgiri Hill. It had retained some of the greenery that had sprouted during the previous monsoon, and looked inviting. It was also, she knew, much cooler there than below. By the time she had left the plain behind and started riding through the woods at the foot of the hill, it had become much darker. Still she pressed on, along familiar paths that Julian and Princess Padmini had shown her. The cooling air fanned her flushed cheeks and restored some of her calm.

But the mood was shattered when her mare whinnied nervously, ears pointing upwards. Thinking that she had been disturbed by an animal running through the trees, Caroline paid no heed until she reared up and then began to gallop away in a frenzy. Caroline hung on, striving to rein in the frightened beast, when a thick jutting branch knocked her off balance so that she fell to the ground, which was strewn with day leaves and branches.

Rising slowly after the momentary but sharp spasm of pain had passed, she called out to the mare at the top of her voice, 'Kripa! Come back at once!' But Kripa had taken such a fright that she fled through the trees in a zig-zag fashion until Caroline was left alone in the silent, darkening woods. She cursed the beast and began walking towards a clearing in the wooded hillside. Branches pulled at her dress and hat, startling her. 'I have been here before,' she told herself, 'there's nothing to fear. But I must get out of the woods before it is completely dark.'

As she was afraid of getting caught in the forest after nightfall, Caroline ran fast, hoping to reach the summer palace before the sun set. Birds flew in flocks towards large trees for shelter, and she heard all round the scuttling sounds of animals running to holes and burrows for the night. Hoping she would meet nothing more than a timid-eyed gazelle or jungle fowl, still she ran, lifting her riding-habit above her ankles, until she approached the top of Devgiri Hill.

The gilt cupola of the temple had been illuminated by a hundred brass lamps so that their combined glitter was reflected below on the long flight of steps and shed an aura of light on the hilltop. The sight urged her to quicken her steps, for there on the terrace of the summer palace she could recall the magical evening spent with Julian Lindsay, the one time that they exchanged neither sharp words nor cold glances, the only time they had been untroubled and happy with each other.

Gaining the top, Caroline turned back to stare down at the city of Vijaypur lying in a parched, ochre-coloured plain, vaguely reminding her of the ochre city of Siena.

Lights had began to twinkle in hovel and mansion alike, but Vijaypur palace was strangely dim, its pinky-grey stone phosphorescent in the starlit darkness. The Residency, shrouded by bougainvillaeas, looked like a miniature Greek temple. 'How I shall miss all this,' she thought as she turned away and walked towards Mahadev Vilas, the summer palace with its twin towers.

Caroline walked through the iron gate and across the vast empty central hall, wondering why it was dark, silent and devoid of servants. A murmur of voices rose from the central terrace, and she followed the sounds, unthinking.

Pran Singh, son of the Maharaja by his second wife, sat on a thickly padded mattress on the floor, silken bolsters and cushions supporting him. A silver hookah was before him, bubbling with aromatic tobacco and glowing charcoal. He held the long pipe of the hookah in his left hand, and studied his right hand as he spoke to the half-dozen men around him.

'My father is dying. Even that garrulous fool, Williams, has given up hope. All those powders and pills have failed to restore him.' His aquiline face curved in a sneer. 'I wonder how much that interfering Englishman suspects?'

'Who would suspect your mother, Your Highness? The Maharaja adores her,' one man said.

Pran Singh's face darkened. 'Loves her, but does not wish her son to be the ruler! No, that honour must go to the first-born,' he said bitterly.

'That is the rule, my boy,' an elderly courtier soothed.

Pran Singh leapt up, his eyes livid like coals. 'I recognise no rules!' he shouted. 'Only old women obey rules! I am my father's favourite, born out of his passion for my mother! So I must inherit his throne instead of that whey-faced ninny!'

'You shall, My Prince, you shall,' another companion assured him.

'I must!' Pran Singh growled. 'And if my father's life has to be sacrificed—well, that cannot be helped!'

'Yes, that is so. The Maharaja became remorseful when he fell ill, and began to talk of his sins. He summoned his chief wife and begged her pardon, and promised that Prince Kamal would succeed him,' the elderly courtier said.

'Treacherous old fool!' Pran Singh shouted. 'After swearing to my mother that I would be the Maharaja!'

The older courtier shook his head. 'These things happen. In any case, your mother has avenged his treachery.'

Pran Singh turned away. How would he ever face these men as their master when they knew that he had connived at the slow poisoning of his father, Sitadevi and Princess Indumati?

'My father may sign a document—or that wily Resident will make him do it. Before that, we must act,' Pran Singh said grimly.

'Everything is in readiness, My Prince. You have but to indicate the time!' his accomplice declared.

'Tomorrow—before the moon rises at midnight—when it is dark and still. My astrologer says that is the best hour for an attack. Now let us have an early meal, and check every point before we go to sleep. Tomorrow I shall spend the day at my dear brother's side, so that he suspects nothing. In fact,' Pran Singh paused to smile, 'I shall, like Prince Bharat of our epic, do homage to my elder brother's slippers rather than sit on his throne.'

A loud burst of laughter greeted this remark, but the

courtiers grew solemn at once. It was not an auspicious analogy, because Bharat had not reigned. It was his elder brother, Rama, who had become king of ancient India.

To lighten the mood, another man clapped his hands. 'I shall tell your servants to bring in the food,' he said to the Prince.

'It is fortunate that the old servants of the palace left for their villages on the order of the Resident! He wished to prevent them from falling sick, as the Tewar party was housed here,' the Prince observed.

'And hastened the end of his plans!' another man said.

'Remember,' Pran Singh spoke slowly. 'The Resident is not to be touched unless he resists. Only my half-brother is to be abducted—by brigands, we shall announce—in return for a ransom. It is a common enough occurrence!'

Caroline felt herself trembling from head to toe. She stifled a wild desire to scream by clapping her icy hand over her mouth, and began to back away, stealthy step on stealthy step, across the hall. It was dark, she thought, and no one would see her. 'I have to get away at once. But how? Should she take the long and difficult route through the dark woods or the quicker, easier one down the flight of stone steps? She debated the matter as she tiptoed through the garden towards the temple and those interminable steps. It was too easy to resist, and the forest filled her with apprehension. Snakes, foxes and wild cats abounded there. Her feet seemed to move of their own volition towards the steps and carried her down them, one by one, towards the safety of the palace. She could feel her heart thudding and the blood pounding in her head as she negotiated the steep flight in silence.

Pran Singh leaned on the terrace balustrade and saw the slim supple figure of a woman as she descended, step by step. He frowned and narrowed his eyes. *'Who is she?'* he wondered, *'And what was she doing here?'* Curious, and also afraid that the stranger might have heard their conversation, he motioned his followers to silence as he leaped over the balustrade and ran across the hillside towards the long stone staircase.

Hearing the sound of running feet, Caroline turned back and looked up. As she did so, the light from the temple cupola glistened on her auburn hair, creating a fiery halo around her pale face. She saw the tall thin figure of Pran Singh, and with a gasp of terror, forced her feet to quicken their pace. He followed in pursuit, not over the steps, but down the hill until he reached her side, barring her way.

Caroline stood before him, her breath coming in shallow gasps, trying to fathom his purpose as he looked at her, calmly, appraisingly. Swiftly she decided that further flight was useless.

'What were you doing near the palace, Miss Saheb?' Pran Singh asked in his low voice.

'I . . . went to pray . . .' she replied unsteadily.

Pran Singh's eyes narrowed. 'I do not believe you. Why should you, a Christian, pray to Parvati?'

'I . . . Sir Julian brought me here once . . . I liked the ceremony,' she muttered.

'Ah, the tolerant, eclectic Resident has wide views! So he initiated you into our ceremonies?'

Pran Singh saw the colour recede from her face and a pulse beat at the base of her throat. He knew, too, from Caroline's terrified expression that she had overheard him. Had it been another woman he might have hesitated, but he could not trust this governess whom he had seen in the Resident's arms and who was a friend of Princess Padmini.

'I regret I must detain you, Miss Saheb,' he said politely.

'Why?' Her voice was hoarse.

'You know why. You heard my plan.' Pran Singh watched her closely and was convinced that she had heard. She was, he thought, a poor actress. 'I will not harm you if you co-operate.'

'Co-operate? How can I do that?' she asked wildly.

Pran Singh smiled. 'No, of course you won't co-operate. You are loyal to the Resident,' he said with a sneer.

Caroline blushed, remembering how Pran Singh had found her in the Resident's embrace on the eve of Prince Kamal's wedding.

'Very well. I shall detain you here and decide what to do,' he said grimly.

'They will look for me if I do not return,' Caroline retorted.

Pran Singh shook his head. 'No, Miss Saheb. They are too busy worrying about my dying father. They will not miss you until . . . it's too late.'

Caroline knew that resistance was useless. She had no option but to obey, whatever the consequences. Nor did she harbour any illusion about a man who could poison his father to gain the throne. Sighing, she began to mount the steps, utterly exhausted. Pran Singh did not touch her, walking behind her in silence.

A chaos of sound greeted her emergence on the hilltop. All six companions of the Prince had been watching the scene avidly and now a babble of voices broke loose. Pran Singh silenced them all with a gesture.

'Paresh,' he said quietly to a middle-aged man built

like a heavyweight. 'Take the lady to a pleasant room above. Let her be comfortable and well fed. She must be guarded all night.'

Paresh Nath, the Prince's wrestler, nodded and led Caroline to the Maharani's suite in the summer palace. She slumped down in the nearest chair and closed her eyes, while Paresh and another accomplice locked the windows and then left her alone, locking her door.

For a long time she sat still, rebelling against her fate; then her anger died down, to be replaced by a dawning realisation that she was in actual danger. Pran Singh, she thought, would not let her return to Vijaypur alive. She would be either killed or taken to a far-off place, left to perish under the cruel summer sun. The latter seemed more likely, because an Indian ruler intent on keeping his throne could not afford to have the murder of an English subject on his hands.

She began to pace the room in extreme agitation, panic mounting within her until she could no longer think clearly. 'Foolish girl,' she chided herself. 'Would it not be better to be drinking tea with Edward, rather than shut up here, facing certain extinction?' The very idea that she would never see her friends again, that she would not be free and alive, threw her into a fit of convulsive tears. 'Am I to perish like this?' she cried out in the lamp-lit room. 'With no one to know what became of me?'

The evening passed into night, hot and palpitant, still and moonlit. Paresh Nath brought her a dish of tandoori lamb cooked in yoghurt and herbs, but the morsels stuck in her throat. The man returned to remove the almost untouched dishes, and went out, re-locking the door behind him.

Caroline had noticed a small writing-desk in the corner of the room, and had idly pulled out one of the drawers. It contained some sheets of paper, which gave her an idea that might work. She sat down and began to pray, her eyes fixed on the gilt cupola of Parvati's temple. As tears of helplessness streamed down her face, she murmured prayers of her childhood. Finally, as exhaustion tugged at her, she lay down on the soft, satin-covered bed and was soon fast asleep.

Next morning, Caroline knew that no one would have missed her at the palace. 'This is the price of keeping irregular hours,' she told herself ruefully. 'If I kept to a strict routine, someone would have wondered where I was.' She got up and went to the large bathroom adjoining the bedchamber. A large marble tub shone invitingly, in readiness for a visitor. She began to prepare for a bath when her glance fell with joyful incredulity on the only window there.

It was large, low and unlocked. Nor were there any grilles, to bar thieves from entering. '*Parvati has heard my prayers*,' she thought exultantly as she splashed water on herself and tidied her dress and hair.

As soon as she returned to the bedroom, the door was open by the wrestler to admit Pran Singh. The Prince was casually dressed in *kurta* and *churidar*, without a hint in his bearing of the momentous action he was contemplating—to seize his father's throne by abducting and killing the rightful heir. He scrutinised his prisoner with satisfaction.

'I have, despite my dislike of them, respected the British for their courage,' he said evenly. 'You strengthen that respect, Miss Saheb.'

'Thank you, Your Highness,' she replied through stiff lips.

'I am going away now. You will remain here. Paresh Nath will bring your meals. Perhaps, if you co-operate, I shall see that you are safely escorted to Bombay and put on board a ship bound for England.'

'What will my . . . co-operation involve?'

Pran Singh smiled. Caroline thought how handsome he would be if he were not so cruel and dissolute.

'You will write to the Resident, telling him that you are disgusted with Vijaypur and wish to escape from its monotony.'

'That is all?' Caroline asked with feigned excitement.

'Yes,' Pran Singh murmured, drawing close to her. He raised a long thin hand and with slow sensuous movements traced the outlines of her arched brows, straight nose, firm chin and rested on the soft curved lips, his opaque eyes fixed on hers.

Caroline wondered if for the sake of everyone concerned she should respond to the mild overtures of the young rake, and try to detain him in her room—perhaps even win her freedom. Instead, she let the crucial moment pass. 'I could never do it,' she thought ruefully. 'Not even if I tried. Did I not try to respond to Edward's hungry kisses? To no avail. He, and this Prince—they all leave me unmoved. There is only one man who can stir me.'

Pran Singh's fingers seemed to float away back to his side. 'Keeping yourself for the great love, Miss Saheb?' he asked mockingly.

Caroline's eyes misted at the futility of it all.

'I hope he is worthy of such devotion,' he continued meaningfully, with a discerning glance at her pale, intense face. 'You need have no fears about me,' he resumed, casting her a disdainful glance, 'I like my women to have more flesh. You are still unripe, like a green mango. And that hair—why it's like fire. Gives me a headache!'

Caroline lowered her eyes to hide the welter of feelings rising within her.

'Is there anything you want—apart from your freedom?' he asked smoothly.

'Yes, Your Highness,' she replied at once. 'Could I have some vermilion powder from the temple?'

Pran Singh frowned. 'Have you really adopted our faith? Or are you trying to pose as an Indian woman with a *bindi* on your forehead?'

'No,' she said meekly. 'I have . . . come to love your Hindu ceremonies, and have a particular devotion to the mother-goddess.'

The Prince shrugged his shoulders and nodded to the wrestler. 'Get her what she wants,' he said, and then turned to Caroline. 'Stay in your room, Miss Saheb, and create no problems. I might still relent in the hour of victory.'

She curtsied meekly as the Prince left her room, and sat down to wait for Paresh Nath.

CHAPTER
SEVENTEEN

CAROLINE AWAITED the arrival of the vermilion powder, striding up and down the room after a while in great agitation. When she paused once in her frantic pacing, she saw that the blazing sunlight had been replaced by an oppressive grey calm. Like a vast dark curtain, clouds began to bank up against the horizon.

'A storm is brewing over the sea,' she thought, and wondered how this would affect Pran Singh's plans. Would the Resident be able to foil the younger prince's bid to usurp the throne? Speculation on these events only heightened her growing restlessness. She felt an angry frustration at being imprisoned at a time when she could have assisted the Resident.

Hearing the sound of hooves, Caroline rushed to the window to see a group of horsemen ride out of the summer palace grounds towards the woods, from where they would take the path to the main palace below. She could see only their retreating figures, not their faces. 'Now that Pran Singh has gone, I must act soon!' she resolved, suppressing the ever-present terror of what might happen. She sat down on the rumpled bed, slowly formulating her thoughts and course of action.

Paresh Nath opened the door shortly after, bringing in a tray of fruit and tea, and a small bowl containing vermilion powder. He paused to glance at the distraught

English girl and said, 'You eat and rest, Miss Saheb. You will feel better then.'

'Yes, I shall do that,' Caroline replied, unable to keep the growing agitation from her voice.

As soon as the door had closed, she leaped from the bed and, going over to the writing-desk, stared at the thick sheets of paper lying unused and dusty. Immediately she took them out, blew the dust off, and began mixing the vermilion powder with hair-oil which she had found among the toilet articles in the bathroom. When it was a smooth paste, she dipped her forefinger in it and began writing a message addressed to Sir Julian Lindsay.

She wrote carefully, to avoid smudging, and was so engrossed in her task that a sudden clap of thunder caused her to jump in alarm. Going to the window, she found that the sky had darkened to a charcoal grey, and a wild wind blew in from the west, swirling dust and dry leaves in a dervish dance. A streak of lightning flashed across the sky, followed by the boom of thunder that seemed to reverberate around the hill.

Caroline returned to the desk and completed the message, then folded it and placed it in an envelope. For a moment she sat motionless, staring at the letter, and then hurried to a closet where several silk saris were lying on a shelf. They were heavy and smelled musty, as if they had been left unused for a long time. She knotted three saris together, and then, going to the bathroom, tied one end of the sari chain firmly to the door-handle. Then she changed from her heavy riding-habit into a deep green sari, carefully, as she had remembered Pannabai draping it round her on the Prince's wedding day. Standing for a moment before the long gilt-framed Belgian mirror, she stared pensively at her reflection, and then hurried back to the bathroom. Throwing open the window, Caroline threw the knotted saris out, and then got out onto the ledge. Murmuring a prayer, she began to slide down the wall of the summer palace, using the sari chain as a rope.

The fierce wind tugged at her clothes and blew at her hair, making her sway during the descent, but it also drowned the sound of her feet grazing the stone walls and the thump of her landing. The imminent storm had driven everybody inside, including the guards who had been marching around earlier in the morning. Caroline pulled the loose end of her sari low over her hair and ran barefoot to the Parvati temple.

Jaydev, the young priest, was preparing for *puja*, arranging marigolds and camellias around the resplendent deity. Coconuts, incense sticks and fruit were waiting on gold plates, ready to be offered as oblations.

'Guruji!' Caroline whispered, as she crept towards him. The young Brahmin turned sharply on his heel, astonished to see a foreign lady.

'You remember me? I came here a month ago with the Resident Saheb!' she said quickly in Hindi. The priest nodded, still bewildered by her presence here.

'Please, Guruji, help me! Take this letter to the Resident Saheb,' she whispered urgently.

Jaydev's calm eyes darted to the envelope she held out in both hands, and back to her again.

'Why do you not take it yourself?' he asked quietly.

Caroline wondered in panic whether he could be trusted with the truth, or was he in league with Pran Singh? The gamble had to be made, so she told him everything. The priest listened in grim silence. Then he reached out for the letter. 'Give it to me. I shall hand it over to the Resident.' He tucked the envelope in the folds of the *dhoti* round his waist and, glancing once at the goddess, closed his eyes in prayer. Caroline sank down on her knees, whispering a prayer of her own, as Jaydev slipped out of the sanctum of the temple and headed for the woods.

Suddenly she raised her head. 'Why am I sitting here? The priest was right . . . Why don't I give it myself . . . No . . . I cannot walk so fast, and I would soon be intercepted . . . But let me at least try!' She sprang to her feet and left the temple as another burst of lightning and thunder split the skies. Quickly, head bent, she began to walk towards the forest path, unaware that the sari-end had slipped from her hair.

Hearing the sound of hurrying footsteps, Caroline broke into a run and, as she did so, the footsteps quickened until they were right behind her. Even as she ran, she knew it was hopeless. In a minute, two hands pulled her back.

'Ah! I might have known by that fire-coloured hair!' Pran Singh said softly. 'I was watching a woman in a dark sari enter the temple,' he explained to one of his companions, 'wondering who it could be. Then, as the woman came out, I saw the hair of fire. And of course I had to get her back!'

Caroline was breathless as she stood staring at Pran Singh. 'Why have you come back?'

'What were you doing in the temple?' he retorted, curious and suspicious.

'I . . . wanted to pray . . . that's why I asked for the vermilion,' she said hastily.

His brown eyes were like agates and just as hard.

'Where is the priest?' he asked, glancing at the unfinished preparations for worship.

'The priest?' Caroline echoed nervously. 'Why, I . . .

expect he must . . .' Her voice trailed away as Pran Singh slowly shook his head.

'I regret you are a liar, Miss Saheb. You have sent word through the priest, haven't you? Failing to charm the Prince, you tempt the priest!' Before Caroline could deny it, Pran Singh snapped his fingers at his companion and jerked his head towards the woods. 'At once! Intercept the priest and lock him up.' He turned back to Caroline, who was utterly spent. 'I have to think of some other penalty for you, Miss Saheb. I cannot believe you any more. Come,' he said, grasping her wrist and dragging her towards the temple.

Outside, a storm raged; the burning day had become a cool evening. Caroline felt herself buffeted by its force as she was led back to the temple. 'Lock her up in the haunted store-room!' he commanded the retainers, who stared wide-eyed at the woman whom they assumed was locked in a palace room.

'What will the ghost do to her if she can escape through locked doors?' one man asked.

Pran Singh rewarded him with a resounding slap. 'Imbecile! Why were you not guarding her? But for me, she would have escaped!' he shouted. 'Now lock her up in that windowless vault. She must not escape again!'

Caroline was shut up in a tiny room used for storing temple treasures. There she had abundant time to reflect on her impending doom. 'The priest will be caught, and Sir Julian will not get my message!' she thought, as fear rose within her. 'And what will become of us all? Prince Kamal will be killed eventually, and so shall I. Who knows what fate awaits Sir Julian!'

Fear turned to an overwhelming misery that every-thing had gone wrong. 'Nothing has worked out,' she said to herself resentfully. 'All my hopes of a new life have turned to dust and ashes!'

Her thoughts were disturbed by the sound of torrential rain beating against the temple walls. For an hour the rain lashed Devgiri Hill and Vijaypur, washing dust-encrusted leaves, moistening the baked soil. Caroline fancied she could almost smell the fragrance of the rain-washed world. As the rain ceased, she heard the sound of gunfire down below. The sound seemed to echo and vibrate on the hilltop. A nameless dread overwhelmed her. So Pran Singh had finally engaged in violence to attain his end! Had he killed innocent men who had stood in his way?

Battling with a wild despair, Caroline sat on the cool stone floor, covering her face with trembling hands, racked by stormy tears. It was as though she had nothing else to live for, nowhere else to go. 'If anything has happened to him . . . I shall not be able to endure it. I have lost home and family, but this loss will be insupportable!'

The rational part of her mind told her that nothing was over. If somehow she could bargain for her freedom and go away with Edward Lockwood, she could begin a new life filled with every comfort. She thought of Edward, his placid, easy-going nature untroubled by introspection. But her eyes played tricks with her. She saw another face, not quite so handsome, but lit by a sharp intellect and a vibrant presence, a face that could be cold and commanding but also tender and ardent. She remembered the deep blue eyes that gazed deep into her, and the chiselled lips that awakened her to passion. She thought of his temper and impatience underneath a courageous and generous nature, and a mind with wide horizons and sympathies.

'Just as well if I did perish,' she told herself. 'I could not bear to live with the knowledge that he rejected me with so little ceremony!'

Now she could hear the sounds of carbines louder and nearer in the rain-washed stillness, reaching up to and echoing against the hill. Gradually the sounds died down, leaving only an ominous silence. Caroline closed her eyes and waited for the inevitable.

It was night when she awoke from a fitful slumber that had done nothing to restore her equanimity or banish her despair. Caroline realised that she had gone to sleep on the floor, and every part of her body ached. The little room was damp, filled with the smell of stored oil-lamps and incense which made her head ache. It occurred to her that her corpse would be found in the temple store-room only many days later.

As Caroline once more scanned the stone walls for a chance of escape, a scraping sound was audible, growing louder and louder until she could discern in the faint light that a large stone slab was slightly moving. Terrified, she shrank against the opposite wall. As the rattling round the slab grew louder, she ran towards the metal door and beat her fists on it. Better to face the guards posted by Pran Singh than this eerie, unknown peril!

'Get me out! Please!' She screamed, nerves stretched to breaking-point as the slab quivered, and then crashed to the stone floor. Slowly she turned round to face the horror that awaited her.

The Resident stood at the caved-in entrance, dressed in the white uniform of the commander of the Vijaypur Lancers. His dark hair glistened with rain-water and the sapphire eyes seemed more vivid against his sunburnt face. He looked at her in her crushed dark-coloured sari, her damp auburn hair plastered to her head, and the large eyes lustreless with fear and anguish.

'Caroline . . .' he murmured in a voice husky with suppressed emotion. 'Are you all right?'

Caroline was too stunned to speak. A wave of relief such as she had never known washed over her. She stood trembling and tearful, gazing mutely at Sir Julian Lindsay, who advanced towards her, arms outstretched, until he folded her in his embrace.

'You are not hurt, my dear?' he asked, pressing her quivering body closer to him, resting her head against his shoulder.

'No,' she murmured hoarsely, as tears, of many emotions welled up in her eyes and flowed from her face to his dusty white tunic. He felt her body racked by sobs, and tightened his arms around her.

'Don't cry, Caroline. It's all over. You are quite safe.'

She raised her face to him. 'I never thought you would come. I thought . . .'

Caroline's words were stopped by Julian's lips closing over hers. He kissed her gently, and then with a wild despair as if time was slipping away. Caroline did not resist. Armed with the full knowledge that this was both a greeting and a goodbye, she responded to him as his lips moved over her lips, throat, shoulders and as he bent his head to rest it in the hollow of her breasts. The fire that lay between them, like a dormant volcano, leaped into life, searing and melting, until they felt their flesh had coalesced into one incandescent glow.

Even after they drew apart, breathless, they clung together in that small room filled with the scents of worship.

A gust of rain-scented air blowing in through the opening roused him. Releasing Caroline slowly, he gazed at her with an enigmatic expression. 'I won't ask your pardon this time,' he said in a wry voice.

'I am not asking you to,' Caroline replied softly. 'I can only thank you for finding me.'

Julian was about to protest and say something, but changed his mind. Instead, he asked briskly. 'Are you fit to ride a horse? I must return to town.'

'Yes, I can. Will you tell me what happened?'

'Certainly—as we go along.'

Darkness had been deepened by the storm. Even now Caroline could see the dull lowering sky over them as Julian led her through the opening in the temple out to the hillside. He held her hand firmly, guiding her across the clearing with the long flight of steps at the edge of the woods. There, his favourite horse, Pakshiraj, stood pawing the ground. Sir Julian loosed him and then helped Caroline up to the saddle and sprang up behind her. The horse set off, nervous and watchful in the darkness, as his master guided him.

'How did you find me?' Caroline asked as soon as they set off. 'Did you get my letter? How did you break open the stone slab?'

'Yes, I got your letter. The priest, Jaydev, brought it to me late in the morning.'

'Ah, so he did reach you! I thought Pran Singh's men would have intercepted him!'

'Jaydev grew up here on the hillside. It would take a very wily man to find him! He told me of the situation, and of course I gleaned much from your letter.' Julian paused. 'That was an ingenious idea of yours—to write with vermilion powder.'

'Necessity makes us clever, I suppose,' Caroline replied, warmed by his appreciative tone. 'You would be surprised if I told you more about my exploits! I actually escaped from a locked room upstairs.'

'Tell me,' he said gently, his hand tightening around her waist as Pakshiraj suddenly stopped, ears strained upward.

Both were silent, and soon realised why. From below, sounds of people were heard—men who were obviously on the run. Instantly Julian dismounted and pulled Caroline down. 'Pakshiraj,' he said in Hindi to the horse, 'Go and wait near the cottage!'

In amazement Caroline watched the horse trot away as he had been ordered. 'We shall go there by a more devious route,' Lindsay explained softly. 'So that the men hear sounds from two different directions. Come now, follow me!'

Caroline stumbled over the stony ground, following the tall figure who pushed aside overhanging branches for her. When they had walked for ten minutes, Julian guided her to a small cottage amid gnarled old trees, whose leaves and branches were still dripping with raindrops.

'We had better wait here until Pran Singh's men are out of the way,' he said in a low tone as they entered the mud-walled, thatched cottage. 'This is where the foresters store wood.'

They sat down on the damp floor after Julian had spread hay over it. It was dark, and they could make out only the outlines of each other. Caroline was overwhelmed by the bittersweet sensation of being alone with Julian on this soft dark night.

Briefly he told her how he was alerted by her letter. He had been anticipating trouble ever since they had discovered that the Maharaja and Sitadevi had fallen ill with opium poisoning, and the information overheard by Caroline enabled him to foil Pran Singh's treachery.

When this ambitious younger prince had invited Kamal to a night's entertainment on Devgiri Hill, the Resident had asked the Crown Prince to pretend that he knew nothing, and so allow Pran Singh to betray himself. The Vijaypur Lancers hid on the densely wooded part of the hill, waiting to seize Pran Singh and his men just as they prepared to 'abduct' the Crown Prince.

'Did you capture Pran Singh?' Caroline asked.

'Yes, and most of his followers. A few escaped . . . You heard them roaming over the hill. They were coming to take you as hostage. We shall round them up in the morning.'

'What will happen to him?'

'He and his mother will be given the choice of exile outside India or imprisonment,' he said grimly. 'Vijaypur must be rid of such corrupt influences.' He paused, and murmured, 'I am glad I found you in time.'

'How did you get here before them?' Caroline asked, shivering with cold and a strange excitement.

'I took another route. The medieval ramparts of the fortress were built along the hills, so I came along that way. Once I reached the summer palace, the servants told me where you had been kept. It would have been difficult to break down the metal door, but I knew of the secret opening in the stonework of the temple.'

'I . . . had given up all hope,' she declared, and heard him laugh softly in the darkness.

'Do you have so little faith in my enterprise and initiative?'

'I didn't know if Jaydev had got the letter to you,' she explained.

'Even before I had met him, a search-party was being organised by seven in the morning, when Pannabai reported that you had not slept in your bed.'

'I see,' Caroline murmured, glad that he could not see her flushed cheeks.

'Do you?' he asked, drawing her closer to him and kissing her lips lightly. 'I am glad I found you,' he said again, in a husky voice. Then slowly he released her and got up, muttering something about starting a small fire as he groped in the dark for a flint-box on the window-ledge.

Perplexed, Caroline tried to see him in the darkness and understand the cause of his change of mood.

'There is no flint,' he said as he sat down again, keeping a safe distance between them. They sat in silence, as it began to rain again.

'Sleep, Caroline,' Julian said. 'I shall wake you as soon as the rain stops. We must get back to the palace soon.'

'I don't feel sleepy,' she replied, looking at him whenever flashes of lightning illuminated the interior of the hut.

'You are remarkably resilient after such a harrowing experience. It is not what one expects in a woman.'

'Have you had many such experiences?' Caroline asked.

'So many!' the Resident said wistfully.

'Tell me about them!'

Julian told her of a few episodes, to while away the time and to keep the barrier of correct behaviour between them. Yet, while they talked, he was overwhelmed by a deep regret that this brave, open-minded and lovely woman could not be his.

Worn out by several wakeful nights, Caroline at last fell asleep. He watched her now in the grey light of dawn, memorising the full curved lips that knew how to laugh and kiss, the nose that expressed disapproval, the chin that never ceased to be stubborn and the closed eyes beneath which lay emerald fires.

Outside, a cool breeze stirred, bringing in the scent of damp earth and wild flowers. Caroline also stirred, and found Julian sitting close by, eyes dark with pain.

'Is it morning already?' she whispered, unable to hide her regret.

He nodded gravely. 'We must go now, Caroline. I assured Lockwood that I would take you back to the palace last night. As it is you are late.' He rose, flinging the damp tunic across his shoulder and brushing back his tousled hair with his hand.

'Late for what?' Caroline asked, alarmed.

His eyes hardened. 'For your departure to Bombay and then England,' he replied, and without another word went out to prepare for their return.

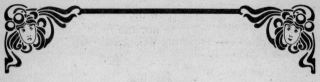

CHAPTER
EIGHTEEN

THE SUMMER squall had passed, leaving Vijaypur fresh and cool for a few days before the hot winds blew in from the Thar desert.

Caroline had finished her evening bath, and was sitting before the mirror while Pannabai dressed her hair in a chignon. Her gown of peacock-blue silk shimmered in the lamp-light. The usually garrulous maid was taciturn today, sensing that Miss Saheb was troubled and unhappy. After adding the finishing touches to Caroline's toilette, she left reluctantly.

With tired eyes, Caroline gazed out of the window at the sunburnt garden and the golden waters of Lake Rashmi in the twilight, struggling with the acute misery that had overwhelmed her ever since Julian Lindsay had announced that she was to leave for Bombay the next day.

'There is no other way,' she said aloud in despair. 'He has made no attempt to stop me. On the contrary, he has been only too eager to arrange my departure with Edward.' An inner voice asked why she had made no attempt to explain, to confess what she felt. Caroline knew the answer to that: she did not wish to be rebuffed and spurned. Her pride could not allow such a humiliation. 'Then why did he show me he cared?' she asked herself, remembering moments of perfect harmony and happiness with him. She knew the answer to that also.

He had neither the time nor the inclination for any deep attachment. Caroline had pieced together fragments of information to learn that he had avoided any emotional involvement. He had had casual liaisons which were pleasant and ephemeral, demanding nothing.

'Very well,' she told her reflection grimly. 'I shall go away, head held high, without betraying my misery.' She left the window and prepared to join the other guests at the new Maharaja's dinner-party.

Shortly after returning to the palace that morning, Caroline had met Sitadevi and learnt of the events which had taken place during her brief absence.

Fearing his end, the Maharaja had summoned his ministers and, in a symbolic gesture of abdication, had handed his ring to the Crown Prince, who became Maharaja Kamal Singh. Pran Singh had been present at the ceremony, and at once set his plan in motion. By then Caroline's letter had reached the Resident, who decided that a time had finally come to reckon with the unscrupulous second prince. Pran Singh's scheme to 'abduct' his half-brother had failed, and he had been taken prisoner. His mother had been imprisoned in the palace until she could be exiled with her son. The old Maharaja recovered, but adhered to his decision to renounce the throne and retire to his hilltop villa at Simla to spend his days in meditation. Sitadevi had offered to accompany him, and was already preparing for departure.

Caroline entered the softly lit drawing-room where the new Maharaja was entertaining the departing British visitor to Vijaypur, the Honourable Edward Lockwood. Other leading British inhabitants had also been invited.

The Resident was in a group of friends, resplendent in white evening dress, medals and decorations, showing no evidence of fatigue after the encounter with Pran Singh or the night spent in a damp forest hut. He stood up when Caroline entered, and after a brief formal greeting resumed his conversation with the Chief Engineer. Edward sat near an open window chatting with Lydia Dalrymple, who frequently fluttered her silk fan and eyelashes.

Seeing Caroline, Edward was at her side instantly. 'Well, Caro, I did not expect to see you looking so composed after a nasty encounter with the cut-throat prince,' he said quietly, his appreciative glance talking in the glory of her auburn hair and simple dress of turquoise silk.

'You seem to have taken my imprisonment calmly,' she said with a touch of asperity.

Edward's grey eyes were inscrutable as he said, 'I had no need to worry. You were in good hands.'

'Yes,' Caroline murmured, unable to hide her confusion, 'I was.'

The colour that suddenly stained her cheeks was not lost on him. 'Have you had enough of adventures, Caro?' he asked in a low voice. 'Or are you happy to leave this godforsaken place?'

She turned away, betraying all that she had sought to conceal.

'So you will miss this place? Well, say your fond farewells tonight after the Maharaja announces our marriage.'

Caroline paled. 'Our marriage?' she whispered, her glance flying to the Resident. 'Why need it be announced? We can . . . just go away . . . quietly after . . . the ceremony.'

Edward's habitual placidity hardly altered at her words, but his shrewd grey eyes seemed to understand. 'Very well, that is how it shall be,' he said, and offered her his arm to take her into dinner.

Dinner was announced by an elegant major-domo. It was the first time that Caroline had been present at an informal dinner given by the Maharaja for the British inhabitants of Vijaypur only. Unlike the gorgeous wedding banquet, everything now was determinedly English from the Spode dinner set, Dunfermline linen and the bland food. But for the weather, it might have been England. The warm, rain-scented breeze and the exotic scent of flowers were manifestly of the tropics.

Caroline sat in the middle, near the young Maharani Indumati, who was still very shy and did not know how to tackle foreign guests. Caroline helped her to carry on a desultory conversation with Mrs Dalrymple. In the interludes of silence which seemed to grow around her, she remembered the first dinner in the same room on the evening of her arrival on a cold January day, of her attempt to champion Princess Padmini, the sneering remarks of ill-fated Prince Pran and the Resident's assurance and dignity. *'Even then, I was drawn to him,'* she thought, concentrating on the floral decorations before her. *'And I had some strange notion that there would be something between us. If only there had not been! I would have returned so happily to England as Mrs Edward Lockwood. Why did I choose to give my heart to a man who held it for a while, nursed my hopes and then extinguished them?'*

She raised her eyes from the decorations and glanced at the Resident, to find him looking pensively at her across the table. He had been laughing and talking a while ago, but now he seemed detached and bemused.

For a long moment they gazed at each other, remembering the first dinner together, until the young Maharaja rose to his feet to toast the health of Victoria, Queen-Empress of India.

The evening seemed to go on for ever. Caroline made half-hearted replies to whatever Edward said, until he, tiring of what he called her dull mood, joined a more lively group led by Miss Dalrymple.

She sat alone, staring out of the long windows into the summer night. A myriad sounds and scents drifted in with a languorous warm breeze. The effect of the storm still prevailed. For a few days the rain-washed freshness would prevail over the dry, gritty summer.

'May I join you, Miss Emerson?'

Caroline turned to find the Resident standing beside her. She nodded, unable to speak, but noting that she was not 'Caroline' but 'Miss Emerson' once more.

'You are very silent tonight,' he said in his deep voice as he sat down.

'I . . . was remembering my first evening here,' she said before she could help it, swift colour flooding her cheeks.

'So was I,' he murmured, surprising her.

'But you are accustomed to it by now, are you not, Sir Julian? So many like me have come and gone!' Caroline's voice quivered on the edge of tears.

He glanced at her, his gaze moving over her auburn hair swept high, at the emerald eyes, the delicacy of her nose and lips, the creamy shoulders and the swell of her breasts where he had once briefly rested his head. Again Caroline blushed, but she did not turn away her tear-threatened eyes. He slowly shook his head with an enigmatic smile.

'No, Caroline, no one like you has come . . . ever,' he said, sadly.

She stared at him, trying desperately to blink back the tears that brimmed dangerously.

'If . . . things could have been different . . .' Julian Lindsay mused in a tone she had never heard before. If there had been any enigma about his sentiments, there was none now in the tender gaze fixed on her. Before Caroline could say anything, he rose abruptly from the brocade sofa by the window. 'Miss Emerson,' he said with courteous formality, since at that moment Edward was approaching them, 'May I take leave of you now? I regret that urgent matters of state will occupy me tomorrow morning when you leave. I wish you . . . every happiness.'

She also rose and curtsied. He turned to Edward and bowed stiffly. 'I wish you . . . all the best, Lockwood . . . and a pleasant journey back to England.' His voice was polite and impersonal.

Edward bowed and shook the Resident's hand, delaying him with inconsequential small-talk until he took the initiative to leave. Throughout the exchange, Caroline stood staring before her with unseeing eyes, as if she was very far away.

When Lindsay had left, Edward turned to Caroline. 'Well, Caro, shall we take a turn in the garden before we retire? We must of course get up early to receive the Reverend Mr Palgrave.'

Nodding acquiescence, Caroline led the way to the garden.

The Resident had never found it so difficult to concentrate as in the young Maharaja's council chambers where Kamal Singh had summoned all his ministers for a policy meeting. The long room was cool enough, as half a dozen fan-bearers waved huge fans made of peacock tails. The silk curtains crackled in the warm breeze coming from the windows, bringing in the scent of blossoming jasmine and camellias. Tall frosted glasses of sherbet were placed before the Resident and every member of the Council, followed by aromatic cups of tea. They spoke with enthusiasm about the necessity to modernise agriculture, extend irrigation facilities, build schools and hospitals. Yet they wondered why the Resident, who had initiated these measures and had been their ardent advocate for so long, was now pre-occupied with his smoking pipe.

'Your Excellency,' the young Maharaja said, turning to address him in the formal manner required at Council meetings. 'May my ministers have an idea of the esti-mates for these schemes?'

The Resident glanced at Kamal Singh, taking a few moments to absorb the question. 'Of course, Your Highness,' he said abruptly. 'Here they are.' He began to read the estimate for each item in a strangely detached voice until the sound of a carriage clattering out of the courtyard and towards the palace gates drowned his voice.

The footmen cried 'Chalo! Jaldi Chalo!' at the top of their voices, enjoining the horses to speed. 'We have to go far away to Bombay!'

He stopped reading for two full minutes, sitting sombre-faced and tight-lipped in the seat opposite the Maharaja. His pipe smouldered at his side, and then became extinguished. The young Maharaja lowered his eyes, frowning, shuffling papers to divert the attention of the elderly ministers, who gazed at the Resident expectantly. They did not guess, neither could they know, the cause of his sudden silence. They thought instead that the Resident Saheb was waiting for the noise of the six cantering horses and four wheels to fade away before he resumed speaking.

The sound of the speeding carriage receded, and silence reigned in the palace grounds once more, broken only by the twitter of birds. A different kind of silence settled in the Resident's heart, without the joy of bird-song. It was reflected, the Maharaja saw, in the darkness of his eyes, which were now hard and stern, and the set lips which threatened never to laugh again.

Resolutely, the Resident turned to the sheaf of papers before him. It was, after all, the beginning of a new era, and the chance for putting his cherished dreams into practice. For long he had envisaged just such an opportunity to experiment and innovate. Here was the chance. In a cold and clear voice he began to describe how Vijaypur could be turned into a modern state.

When the council meeting ended, even the most orthodox and suspicious councillor was won over by the Resident's visionary schemes. It was a moment of triumph for him after three years of struggling to win support for plans to modernise this feudal state. Yet, as he left for the Residency, there was no sense of elation in him. The ministers watched, puzzled. Only his friend, the young Maharaja, understood, and murmured that Englishman had a strange way of conducting their private lives.

It was the longest day he could remember, longer than the days of the seige of Meerut or Cawnpore during the Mutiny. With the recollection of the Mutiny, Lindsay thought of Priscilla, the fragile bride he had lost during those turbulent months. But had he felt as utterly bereft as he did now? There had always been, he thought, challenges to be met and new frontiers to be discovered, with no need for love. Casual dalliances had sufficed in the interlude of work. *'Now everything seems empty and meaningless,'* he thought. *'Not all the success in my work or even its fulfilment will bring me the happiness I felt in Caroline's presence.'*

To shake off the mood of gloom that engulfed him, he went to have dinner with the Dalrymples, where Lydia fatigued him with her adoration. He returned home in an even darker mood, and thought a boat-ride across the lake to the villa would calm his restlessness.

Lotus Mahal floated like a huge lustrous pearl on the silvered waters of Lake Rashmi. A late moon had risen in the cloudless sky, turning everything to pale gold. Every tower of the main palace, the curved balconies of the lake villa, every ripple of the lake and the cupola of the hilltop temple stood out clearly in this light. It was well past midnight; the town was asleep and no lamps burned in the palace.

Reaching the villa, Lindsay went up the marble stairs that led to the curved terrace from where one could see the sweeping vista of Vijaypur. Suddenly he stopped. A woman sat on the terrace, willowy and graceful in a flowing dress, the moonlight silvering her bare arms, face and her hair. He remembered that Lotus Mahal was believed to be haunted by the ghost of a Maharani who had met a lover here, only to be drowned by the Maharaja. *'Absurd!'* he chided himself, as he walked purposefully forward. Moonlight, he knew, played tricks with one's vision. Once in a Bengali village he had seen six veiled women bowing to him at the edge of a paddy-field. They had turned out to be several banana trees waving in the moonlit breeze.

Then, as he was close upon her, Julian felt his heartbeat quicken. Had he seen a ghost at last? He passed a hand across his eyes and walked slowly until he stood beside her.

'Caroline!' he cried, incredulous, snatching up her hands in his.

'Yes, Julian?' came the gentle response.

'I thought you had left with . . .' Julian's voice sounded unsteady even to himself.

'When the time came, I could not leave,' she said gravely. 'Edward understood. In fact he said he had expected me to stay behind.'

'Why did you stay, Caroline?' he asked, his hands now on her shoulders, his eyes gazing down into her moonlit ones. 'He had so much to offer you . . . Why did you refuse?'

For a moment Caroline's eyes seemed dark and fathomless like Lake Rashmi. Then a familiar fire danced in them. 'I wanted to go on being a governess,' she said, laughing softly.

'I thought you wanted to be a Countess,' Julian replied.

'How could you think that? Is that why you became so harsh and aloof?'

'Do you blame me?' said Julian, gazing up at the temple spires on Devgiri Hill glimmering in the moonlight. 'That evening on the hill I knew that I could not live without you, and intended to ask you to become my wife as soon as the two weddings were over. On the very evening when I was going to speak, the Honourable Edward Lockwood arrived and announced his plan to marry you.' He looked at Caroline. 'I was both angry and astonished that you had encouraged me to hope, when you were engaged to Lockwood.'

'How could you believe me to be so false? Did I not

betray my feelings for you?' she asked sadly.

Julian drew her close, gazing into her eyes. 'I feared that I had misunderstood your sentiments . . . or that, despite your sentiments, you preferred the comfortable and carefree existence Lockwood offered.'

'I admit that the prospect of becoming a Countess did tempt me at first,' Caroline murmured, her eyes twinkling. 'But after serious consideration I decided that you were more eligible . . . as a possible Viceroy of India.'

Julian frowned for only a moment, until he saw the familiar sparkle in her eyes. They both began to laugh, and the sound of their laughter floated over the diamond ripples of the lake, flew to the twin towers of Lotus Mahal and finally reached to the luminous sky. As the sounds of laughter faded, he drew her closer and murmured, 'Why are you determined to torment me, my love?'

'To punish you for the hours of misery you caused me,' Caroline whispered.

'What about the days of misery you gave me? What reparation will you make for them?' Julian asked tenderly.

Caroline stood on tiptoe and raised her face to him. 'All my life will be spent in making you happy,' she said softly. 'Is that an adequate atonement, my dearest?'

'Very adequate,' Julian murmured, and bent his head to kiss his future wife.

They felt as if they had melted and merged with one another, losing their separateness in that consuming yet tender embrace. Everything around them seemed to will that incandescent joy which possessed them—the radiant lake and sky, the heady aroma of flowers and the deep silence of the moonlit night.

'My darling,' the Resident of Vijaypur whispered,

releasing Caroline, 'It is time we left. I have to rise early and request the long-suffering Mr Palgrave to marry us as soon as he can. Your reputation must be tarnished after these nocturnal rendezvous with me on hilltops and lakesides.' He paused to glance at her questioningly. 'You will not mind a quiet ceremony?'

'No time to make a wedding dress?' Caroline asked playfully.

'I cannot wait,' he replied, and walked over to the flower-beds where jasmine and camellias bloomed. He plucked several of the blossoms and handed them to Caroline. 'At least you will not lack a wedding bouquet,' he said gently, 'made of flowers as exquisite and resilient as yourself.'

Caroline bent her head to breathe in their fragrance, her heart full.

'Come, Caroline,' Julian said, looking at the paling sky touched by lilac and grey, 'Dawn will break soon.'

They went arm in arm to the little boat that waited to cross the waters and take them to a new day and a new life together.

Mills & Boon

Your chance to step into the past
Take 2 Books
FREE

Discover a world long vanished. An age of chivalry and intrigue, powerful desires and exotic locations. Read about true love found by soldiers and statesmen, princesses and serving girls. All written as only Mills & Boon's top-selling authors know how. Become a regular reader of Mills & Boon Masquerade Historical Romances and enjoy 4 superb, new titles every two months, plus a whole range of special benefits: your very own personal membership card entitles you to a regular free newsletter packed with recipes, competitions, exclusive book offers plus other bargain offers and big cash savings.

AND an Introductory FREE GIFT for YOU. Turn over the page for details.

**Fill in and send this coupon back today
and we will send you**

2 Introductory Historical Romances FREE

At the same time we will reserve a subscription to
Mills & Boon Masquerade Historical Romances for
you. Every two months you will receive Four new,
superb titles delivered direct to your door. You
don't pay extra for delivery. Postage and packing is
always completely free. There is no obligation or
commitment – you only receive books for as long as
you want to.

**Just fill in and post the coupon today to MILLS & BOON
READER SERVICE, FREEPOST, P.O. BOX 236, CROYDON,
SURREY CR9 9EL.**

**Please Note:- READERS IN SOUTH AFRICA write to
Mills & Boon, Postbag X3010,
Randburg 2125, S. Africa.**

FREE BOOKS CERTIFICATE

**To: Mills & Boon Reader Service, FREEPOST, P.O. Box 236,
Croydon, Surrey CR9 9EL.**

Please send me, free and without obligation, two Masquerade Historical Romances, and
reserve a Reader Service Subscription for me. If I decide to subscribe I shall receive,
following my free parcel of books, four new Masquerade Historical Romances every two
months for £5.00, post and packing free. If I decide not to subscribe, I shall write to you
within 10 days. The free books are mine to keep in any case. I understand that I may cancel
my subscription at any time simply by writing to you. I am over 18 years of age.

Please write in BLOCK CAPITALS.

Signature _____

Name _____

Address _____

_____ Post code _____

SEND NO MONEY — TAKE NO RISKS.

Please don't forget to include your Postcode.

*Remember, postcodes speed delivery. Offer applies in UK only and is not valid
to present subscribers. Mills & Boon reserve the right to exercise discretion in
granting membership. If price changes are necessary you will be notified.*

4M   Offer expires December 31st 1985

EP9M